A HOLIDAY STORY COLLECTION

TERA LYNN CHILDS

Myths and Mistletoe

Fearless Alchemy
2232 South Nellis Boulevard, Suite 112
Las Vegas, NV 89104

fearlessalchemy.com

This is a work of fiction. Names, characters, businesses, places, events and incidents are either the products of the author's imagination or used in a fictitious manner. Any resemblance to actual persons, living or dead, or actual events is purely coincidental.

ISBN 978-0-9977503-0-0 (ebook)
ISBN 978-0-9977503-1-7 (hardcover)
ISBN 978-0-9977503-2-4 (paperback)

For you, dear reader,
because you make these stories
worth writing

CONTENTS

OF SOLSTICE DREAMING

A DARKLY FAE STORY

ONE

December 20, 9:38 pm

THE MORAINE PALACE was never more beautiful than during the Winter Solstice celebration. Rows of bright, welcoming candles glowed in every window sill and along the jagged parapet of the roof line. Swags of evergreen boughs hung over the window and doors, which had been thrown wide to let nature in and heat out. Sounds of music and merriment drifted out into the night.

Winnie could imagine herself standing at one of those open windows, bathed in the glow of candlelight, eating a fresh winterberry cake and singing songs of Brighid, the goddess of fire, and Cernunnos, the god of the forest.

She couldn't wait to attend in real life.

In the years since her Gran died and passed on the power to see the fae realm in her dreams, Winnie spent most of her waking hours longing for the magical world to be real. A few short months ago she learned it was. What she saw while she slept—people, places, events—was actually happening within the veil.

That only made her long for it more.

She longed for Winter Solstice most of all.

Winnie had dreamed this celebration many times over the years. A three-night festival to celebrate the dead of winter and the promise of a bountiful spring to come. Always watching from a distance, never really there.

The celebration would be different this year for many reasons. Partly because the Moraine had defeated and dispatched the traitor who had threatened to destroy them from within. Partly because their alliance with the Deachair promised to improve the defenses of both clans and give some ease to the mounting concern that war might break out in the realm at any moment.

But mostly, for Winnie at least, this Solstice would be different because she would actually get to attend. In real life. In real time. At the side of her boyfriend, Prince Cathair.

Winnie knew it was a selfish thought. She should be happier for the clan's reasons than her own.

"After tonight," she promised herself. "I'll put the clan first."

As a future princess, it would be her duty.

Winnie shivered in anticipation as she walked the winding forest path that led to the palace door. Tonight was going to be truly magical.

She could barely contain her excitement.

A trio of young fae girls came running toward her on the path, winterberry cakes cupped in their small hands, giggling with pure joy. Winnie moved to step out of the way, but the girls seemed not to notice. As they approached, one reached for another's cake, sending her twisting to the side. Sending her crashing into Winnie.

Only there was no crash.

The girl passed straight through, running and laughing as if Winnie wasn't even there.

Because she wasn't.

Winnie smiled with a heavy sigh.

Sometimes the dreams were harder to discern from the reality. Before she learned the fae realm was real, that her dreams were real, Winnie had never confused the two. Now that she knew, it had become next to impossible for her to tell the difference. Especially since she had been spending more and more time within the veil.

Such was the curse of an *aislingeach*. A curse that Winnie gladly carried if it meant being able to see into the fae realm in her dreams. If it meant being able to help Cathair and the Moraine on occasion. If it meant being able to see him and sometimes even interact with him when she was back in the human realm.

Determined not to miss out on the celebration, even if she wasn't there in reality yet, Winnie continued down the path. A dream Solstice was better than no Solstice at all.

The moment she stepped inside the palace, her senses were overwhelmed. The interior glowed like a fire, lit up by candles on every available surface. The scent of fragrant evergreen filled the air with an aroma that reminded Winnie of Christmas with her grandmother.

She had been gone for more than five years now, but the sense memory was still fresh.

And the music. There was so much music that the very walls of the palace seemed to vibrate with the merry sounds.

Following the music to its source, Winnie wove her way through the crowd, into the ballroom. From her position at the top of the staircase, she could see everything. The fae couples dancing, swirling and moving around the room in a pattern that seemed both chaotic and choreographed. The long table laden with treats and refreshment. The sea of glitter that floated just below the ceiling, with a little help from some fae magic.

It took her breath away.

Winnie scanned her gaze over the room, searching for the tall fae with black and silver hair. It didn't take her long to find him. Cathair stood in the corner of the ballroom, looking very regal in his formal uniform. He was scanning the room much as Winnie had been. Checking on his brother, if she had to guess.

At that moment, Prince Aedan danced by, his girlfriend Bree held close in his arms. Nothing but joy and happiness in his expression. No trace of the darkness that haunted him—that haunted them all.

They had all been touched by Ultan's evil.

Even from this distance, even through the tenuous connection of the dream, Winnie felt the tension leave Cathair's body.

Every cell in her body wanted to cross the room, to be at Cathair's side and wrap her arms around his waist. Even if she wasn't there in reality, she could embrace him in spirit.

The blare of an alarm clock tugged at her consciousness. Time to go.

She gave Cathair one last fleeting look before allowing herself to wake up. That night, after years of dreaming, she would get to experience the celebration for real. The thought almost made it bearable to leave the dream.

TWO

December 21, 3:37 pm

WINNIE RACED up to her room full of excited energy. Most afternoons, at least those after a day at school, she could barely drag herself up the stairs.

Today was different. Today had been the last day of school before winter break. Which meant tonight she would get to attend the Winter Solstice celebration. Finally!

She bounded upstairs, taking them two steps at a time.

Hurrying to get ready, Winnie took a quick shower—the fae realm had many magical qualities, but indoor plumbing wasn't one of them.

She did her best at styling her hair and applying her makeup. She could have left it all natural, knowing that Queen Eimear would have the palace beauty staff ready and waiting. But every minute spent being fussed over meant one less minute enjoying the celebration

Finally, she changed into the beautiful green dress that

Cathair had commissioned for her from a Morainian seamstress. It made her feel like she was already a princess.

On her way out of the room, she checked herself in the mirror. She didn't have the ethereal beauty of the fae, but she looked ready to experience her first Winter Solstice.

Winnie found her aunt in the kitchen, baking. That wasn't surprising. She almost always found Aunt Maureen in the kitchen, baking. Especially that time of year. As a professional pastry chef, the winter holidays were her second-busiest season, after the summer wedding rush.

"Happy Solstice," Winnie said as she entered the kitchen.

Her aunt looked up from a big red mixing bowl. Winnie bit back a smile at the smudge of molasses on her aunt's cheek.

"Happy Solstice," Maureen replied with a smile. "You look beautiful. What's on the schedule?"

Winnie crossed to the stove and poured herself a mug of hot cider from the pot that was almost always simmering on the stove in the cold and rainy winter months.

"The Feast of Brighid is tonight." She inhaled the intoxicating scent of cinnamon and spice. "It's a huge, multi-course dinner followed by a formal ball that lasts all night."

Setting her mug down on the counter, Winnie spun so that the skirt of her dress swirled around her like a cloud.

Maureen went back to her mixing. "Are you staying the night?"

"The festivities run into the wee hours." Winnie stopped spinning. "It just makes sense."

Aunt Mo didn't love it when Winnie stayed in the veil. But Winnie didn't love it that Maureen had kept the truth of their family's magic a secret all those years. In some moments, she was angry at Gran, too, for keeping the secret and at her mom for dying before she could tell Winnie the truth. None of that anger made anything better.

Besides, Maureen was the only family she had left. Winnie didn't like upsetting her.

Meeting Cathair had done a lot to soften her aunt's stance on spending time in the veil. That and Winnie's promise to, even though she and Cathair planned to get engaged, still start college next year.

Future princess or not, Winnie knew that her education was too important to abandon.

"Do you need the car?" Winnie asked. "I can't bike in this dress."

"I have a delivery first thing in the morning," Maureen said, dusting her hands on the sky blue apron dotted with snowflakes that hung around her neck. "I'll drive you to the forest."

"Please and thank you."

Maureen nodded absently as she placed a damp towel over the mixing bowl.

Winnie finished the rest of her cider in a big, heart-warming gulp.

By the time they were on their way, Winnie could barely contain her excitement. Her mind replayed all of the Winter Solstice feasts she'd dreamed before.

"You would be amazed by some of the baked goods the palace kitchen produces." Winnie closed her eyes and pictured the dessert table from last year. "Cakes that touch the ceiling. Sugar bubbles that literally float on air. Truffles that make your skin sparkle."

Maureen laughed. "Some days I wouldn't mind having a bit of fae magic in my pantry."

"Are you sure you don't want to come?" Winnie spun to face her. "Cathair can perform the unshielding spell again. You would love it."

Aunt Maureen's one and only visit to the veil had been eventful, to say the least. Which possibly explained some of her reluctant feelings about the fae realm. Winnie had been trying unsuccessfully to get her to go back ever since.

"I wish I could, sweetie." She steered the car into the trail-head parking lot closest to the veil. "But those fruitcakes aren't going to bake themselves."

Winnie was disappointed but not surprised.

"You know how to reach me if you change your mind?"

Maureen shuddered. "I'm terrified of those ravens."

"They're harmless," Winnie insisted, although she was always a little wary around them herself. "If you need me for anything, they're the only way to communicate with the palace from the human realm."

"I'll use them if I need them."

Winnie leaned across the car and gave her aunt a big hug. "I'll see you tomorrow."

"You want me to pick you up?"

"No, that's okay. Cathair will arrange transportation."

"Here, take my sweater." Maureen reached into the back seat. "You'll freeze half to death."

Winnie loved her aunt, but just then she was too eager to get to the palace to wait any longer. She thanked her aunt for the sweater before jumping out of the car and heading into the forest.

Over the last few months, since the night Cathair first showed her the veil was real, she had walked this path dozens of times. She knew it better than the route from her house to her school. It was carved into her memory.

Tonight, the forest felt different. Full of energy. It was almost as if the very air around her was charged with electricity.

No, not electricity. Magic.

The magic of Winter Solstice. It was all around her. In the way the birds sang brighter, the way the trees rustled sharper, the way the air smelled fresher.

The entire forest was primed to celebrate the darkest day of the year.

Winnie could relate.

She hurried along the path, eager to cross into the veil as quickly as possible because Cathair would sense when she did. Their connection was that strong. It would only be a matter of moments before Cathair appeared at her side.

As she entered the ever-darker depths of the forest, a heavy feeling settled into her stomach. She had long since gotten over her fear of the woods. This was different. Not fear, but unease.

"Must be the hot cider," she guessed. "Shouldn't have downed it so quickly."

But as she drew closer and closer to the veil itself, the feeling grew. Soon, her entire body shook with it. Something was wrong, and that worried her.

When she reached the small clearing where the path passed into the veil, Winnie fought the overwhelming urge to purge her cider onto the forest floor.

Whatever was happening, she wouldn't let it stop her.

She closed her eyes and took a few deep breaths. Gradually, the sensation faded to dull nausea. She could deal with that.

Eyes open, she took a step forward and prepared to pass through the veil.

She crashed into what felt like a solid wall. Winnie blinked several times, trying to clear her vision. She placed her hands before her and tried again.

Again, she ran into a solid surface that wasn't there. Or one that wasn't visible anyway.

It could only be the veil.

Winnie's hands reached out and felt the pulsating energy of it, a dark magic designed to keep curious humans out of the fae realm.

The veil wasn't an actual barrier. It drove humans away with fear. It shouldn't have been able to keep her out physically. If she was able to overcome her fear, entry should have been easy.

The fear hadn't bothered her much since the first time she approached the veil on her own. With the spell of acceptance that Cathair had cast on her, she wasn't supposed to be affected by the dark magic at all.

Judging from the nerves bubbling in her stomach, the spell must have worn off.

But still, it should not have been a physical barrier.

Maybe the realm had instituted stronger security for some reason. Winnie hadn't dreamed of any new threats. Since Ultan's defeat, tensions in the veil had been relatively low. Liam and Tearloch, the heads of the Palace Watch and Royal

Guard were the nervous kind, though. They might have increased protections for the holidays, just in case.

Maybe she needed someone to escort her in.

"Hello?" Winnie called out into the seemingly empty forest. "Regan? Liam? Anyone?"

The Morainian guard patrolled this area of the forest. One of them should have been within earshot. They stood watch, ever at the ready to protect their clan from intruders.

And yet, there was nothing. No one. No guards. No fae. Nothing.

Winnie wasn't sure whether to be annoyed, upset, or worried. She settled on a combination of all three.

Not knowing what else to do, she sat down on a fallen tree and waited for someone to come by.

THREE

December 21, 5:53 pm

WINNIE PULLED her coat tighter around her waist and fought against the escalating shivers. The forest was damp and cold. She wasn't sure how much longer she could wait out here. It was a long walk back home, but freezing to death just outside the veil wasn't exactly her idea of a fun Solstice celebration.

A rustling sound caught her attention. Prepared for it to be another deer or raccoon or random forest beast, she glanced in the direction of the noise.

Moments later, her best friend stepped into view.

Winnie jumped to her feet. "Mel!"

Mel's eyes widened.

"Win, what are you doing out here?" she asked. "I thought you were going in right after school."

"I was," Winnie said. "I am." She walked over to the veil and pressed her hand into the still-solid defense. "I can't."

Mel scowled. "Why not?"

"I have no idea. I've tried everything."

"Did you call for a guard?"

"No one came."

Mel's scowl deepened. "Tearloch would have come."

Winnie gave her a helpless gesture. They all would have come if they'd heard her. Which Winnie had reasoned could only mean that they couldn't. The fae within the veil couldn't hear her at all.

She didn't pursue those thoughts any further because she didn't want to think about the reasons they might not be able to hear her. Some of them were innocuous, but others would be worrisome.

Winnie was ready for a magical celebration. She wouldn't let herself get upset until it became unavoidable.

"You try," Winnie suggested. "See if you can cross through."

A simple test, but one that would eliminate some possibilities.

With a shrug, Mel stepped up to the veil, hesitating only briefly before stepping through.

The moment Mel passed into the fae realm, she disappeared. Like some magic trick. Only this wasn't a trick; it was true magic.

A tiny spark of hope ignited in Winnie's chest. If the problem was a temporary malfunction of magic, it was just a matter of time before the problem corrected itself. It had only been seconds since she tried, but it might only take seconds to fix. Maybe it was working now. Maybe she could finally pass through.

But one step in the direction of following Mel doused the hopeful spark. The veil still wouldn't let her through.

Mel reappeared at Winnie's side. She looked from Winnie to the veil and back again.

"That's weird," Mel said. "Right?"

Winnie fought the burn of tears. It *was* weird. It had never happened before. The first hint of real fear settled into her stomach. She ignored it. They didn't know anything about what was happening. She wouldn't panic. Yet.

"I couldn't even see you," Winnie said. "When you stepped through, you vanished."

Because she had the sight, Winnie could see through the veil. The same magic that let her see fae in their true form gave her the power to see into their world.

Winnie stared at the spot where Mel had walked into the fae realm and disappeared. As if the invisible barrier might reveal some answers.

"Has anything like this ever happened before?" Mel asked.

"No," Winnie said, shaking her head. "Never. Nothing like this."

Mel frowned and then stepped back into the veil. "Can you hear me?"

"Yes, perfectly."

Mel stepped back through. "But you couldn't see me?"

Winnie shook her head, squeezing her hands into fists to fight the push of tears. She hadn't felt so helpless since the time she'd first had to face the veil on her own, when Cathair's life was at risk.

She knew the stakes today weren't high enough to warrant tears. Missing out on a holiday party was hardly the end of the world. But the underlying fear that something was really wrong—that somehow her powers weren't working anymore—had her more than a little worried.

"Hey," Mel said, taking on that uncomfortable tone she got when Winnie got emotional. "We'll get this figured out. Don't freak out."

"I'm not," Winnie lied.

Mel gave her an are-you-kidding look.

"Fine, I am a little," Winnie replied. "What if we can't fix it? What if…."

She clenched her fists tighter until her nails dug into the flesh of her palms. She couldn't even finish the thought out loud. But it finished in her mind just fine.

What if she'd lost her powers?

Falling in love with a fae prince had meant a lot of changed plans. What if those plans were suddenly in jeopardy?

She felt Mel's hands tighten around her shoulders. "I'm sure it's just a magical glitch," she said with such certainty that Winnie actually believed her. "We'll fix this. I promise."

Winnie gave her the strongest smile she could manage.

"Hey, I'm the daughter of a god, remember?" Mel teased. "I can make impossible things happen."

This time Winnie's smile was more genuine. If any two people could solve this problem, Mel and Cathair could.

Mel had the tenacity to take on anything. And, as she pointed out at every opportunity, they had recently learned that she was the daughter of a fae god. They were still testing the extent of her powers.

Cathair would go to the ends of the earth to secure their

future—his and Winnie's. He would not rest until the problem was solved.

Winnie nodded. "That's true."

"Are you okay?" Mel asked. "Are you warm enough?"

Winnie squeezed tighter into her aunt's sweater, wishing for the thousandth time that she'd thought to wear more layers.

"Yeah, I'm fine," she insisted.

Mel looked skeptical. She unwrapped the bright orange scarf from around her neck and slung it over Winnie's shoulders.

Winnie nuzzled into the warmth.

"I'm going inside to get help," Mel said. "I'll get Cathair, and he'll know what to do."

Winnie gave her friend a grateful smile. "Thanks."

Mel hugged her. Then, without another word, she turned and stepped through the veil.

Despite Mel's reassurance, Winnie felt the tears well in her eyes as she shivered against the winter air.

FOUR

December 21, 6:29 pm

Winnie didn't have a watch, and she'd started leaving her phone at home because there was zero signal in the fae realm. But she didn't need a clock to tell her it was getting late. The sun had reached the horizon and was fast disappearing from view altogether.

Soon, it would be dark. What was taking Mel so long?

Don't want to be late...

"Hello?"

Winnie spun around, looking for the source of the whispered words. They had been faint, barely audible above the wind rustling through the trees. She didn't see anyone. She took a few steps in the direction she thought it came from. But when there were no more whispers, she returned to the clearing.

Whoever it was, they had moved quickly.

Winnie didn't want to stray far from the spot where Mel would come looking for her. The last thing she wanted was to get lost in the forest.

…whole plate of purple berryfruit…

"Hello?" Winnie called out again. "Is someone there?"

She didn't hear or see any signs of movement.

The voice was so soft that she couldn't tell if it was male or female, young or old. She stared hard in the direction it seemed to come from. In the fading light, she could barely see a few feet into the dense woods. There was no sign of the source.

Clearly, the cold and rising panic were getting to her. She was starting to hear things.

If Mel didn't get back soon, Winnie was going to have to head home.

She started a mental countdown. One-hundred. Ninety-nine. Ninety—

"She can't get through at all?"

Winnie recognized that voice. She jumped to her feet. "Cathair!"

"She's right out here," she heard Mel say.

A moment later, Mel emerged from the veil. Winnie watched the empty space behind her, relieved when Cathair stepped through. She could see him. In the panic that ate at her while she waited, she'd started to worry that she wouldn't have her sight power anymore.

But she could see him. Everything would be okay.

Winnie rushed toward her love, eager to wrap her arms around him and to feel his reassuring arms around her.

But she froze in her tracks when he asked Mel, "Where is she?"

Winnie waved her hand in front of Cathair's face. "I'm right here."

He looked through her; as if she wasn't there. As if he didn't see her. As if he hadn't heard her.

"Mel?" Winnie couldn't keep the terror from leaking into her tone.

Mel walked to her side. "She's right here." Mel patted Winnie on the shoulder. "Right. Here."

Cathair looked in Winnie's direction. At her, but not *at* her. A frown creased his forehead.

"Mel?" Winnie's voice cracked.

"You can't see her?" Mel asked Cathair.

He shook his head.

Winnie stepped forward, closer to Cathair. Almost afraid of what she would feel—or not feel—Winnie raised her hand and reached out. Her fingers trembled as she pressed her hand against Cathair's chest.

Relief flooded her as she felt the heat of his body, the smooth fabric of his shirt, the steady beat of his heart. She could feel him. She could see him. Those had to be good signs.

He reached up and placed his hand over hers. Only instead of resting on her hand, his palm sank through the space her hand occupied to rest on his own chest.

As if she were nothing more than air.

"I—" Cathair began, then tilted his head and began again. "Is she touching me?"

"I am," Winnie cried.

"Yes," Mel answered. She pointed at the space that both of their hands occupied. "Right there."

"I can… I sense her presence. It's like I *feel* her, but I cannot feel her." He clenched his fist against his chest. "You can see and hear and feel her?"

Mel nodded. "All of the above."

It was strange seeing both of their hands taking up the same space. As Winnie stared at it, it was like her vision wavered from one to the other. One instant she saw her own hand, the next his. It was unsettling.

She slowly withdrew her hand from his chest.

"Ask her to describe what happened," he told Mel.

"Ask her yourself," Mel replied. "She can hear you."

Cathair nodded. "Of course." He stared forward, like he was trying to look where he thought she stood, and asked, "Tell me what happened."

Winnie recounted everything that had occurred since she woke up the morning, from attending the last day of school before winter break to the car ride conversation with Aunt Maureen to walking up to the veil and not being able to get through. Mel relayed every detail, word for word.

"Did you see any unusual animals on your journey?" he asked when she finished. "Perhaps a fae in *la ainmhi* cast a trickster spell on you."

"Not that I can remember," Winnie said, and Mel repeated. "Just the standard songbirds and forest critters."

"It could be the result of contact with a fae portal," he suggested. "Did you step in any shimmering water?"

She shook her head, and Mel told him no.

He went through a series of questions. *Did she step in a field of flowers arranged in a perfect circle? Had she angered anyone who might have witchly powers? Did she bathe in a mountain spring during the last new moon?*

The answers to all of them were no. To Winnie's knowledge, nothing unusual had happened since her last visit to the veil several days ago.

His questions ran out, and they all fell silent. The longer the silence stretched, the more Winnie began to despair. She had truly believed Cathair would know the answer. That as soon as Mel brought him back, he would perform some simple magic to fix things, and she would go about the rest of the day as planned.

But it seemed like he was just as lost and confused by the situation as she was.

What was supposed to be one of the most wonderful nights of the year had quickly turned into one of the worst.

Winnie had thought that losing her powers altogether was the worst thing she could imagine. She was wrong. This was infinitely worse. Being able to see Cathair, to hear him, to even *feel* him, but not being able to actually be with him was torture. She felt like her heart was disintegrating inside her chest. It was getting harder to breathe, and she couldn't stop the sobs that began to shake through her.

"Please don't cry, Winnie," Cathair said in a tone so soft that it only made her cry harder.

"Can you hear her?" Mel asked.

He shook his head. "I can feel her despair."

For some reason, that shook Winnie out of her self-pity. It

was bad enough for her to be scared and upset, but she didn't need to transfer that to Cathair.

She couldn't lose hope. Their connection was still there. This—whatever this was—wouldn't separate them. It wasn't just about Solstice. It was about their future and, magic or not, they would find a way.

FIVE

December 21, 7:32 pm

THE CLEARING WAS GETTING CROWDED. After coming up empty on what might be going on, Mel and Cathair decided they needed additional help. The more minds working on the problem, the better. Mel waited with Winnie while Cathair returned to the palace to bring reinforcements.

He came back with Liam and Tearloch, the heads of the Royal Guard and the Palace Watch who also happened to be his best friends.

"Perhaps someone has cast an invisibility curse," Tearloch suggested.

A curse? Winnie hadn't considered that.

"Is that even possible?" Mel asked.

"It is," Liam conceded. "But curseworks are forbidden magic."

"That doesn't mean some troublemaker wouldn't use it," Tearloch argued.

Mel frowned and shook her head.

"No, but such magics are ancient," Cathair said. "Who would even know how to perform such a spell anymore?"

Tearloch's hands clenched into fists. "I can think of one."

All eyes turned to Cathair. Not because he had that power, but because his brother had been held captive by the one who did.

Winnie's heart beat into her throat.

"Ultan is gone," Cathair said slowly, methodically, as if trying to reassure himself along with everyone else. "Even he is not powerful to reach out from the Everdark."

That declaration quieted the group for a while. Winnie couldn't guess what was going through the others' minds, but hers raced. What was going on? Had she somehow caused it? Could she fix it?

She was making herself crazy.

"Are we sure Mel's not hallucinating?" Tearloch finally asked.

Liam took a step toward Tearloch. "What are you suggesting?"

He and Mel had been seeing each other for a few months, and clearly, he felt the need to defend her. Mel had always been able to take care of herself, though. Even before she learned about the godly blood coursing through her veins.

Mel wrapped her hand around his arm to pull him back.

"She is not," Cathair insisted with a sharp tone. He placed a palm on Liam's chest to push him away from confrontation. "I can sense Winnie's presence."

None would dare to argue with their prince.

"Could she be in a parallel realm?" Liam asked.

"Para-what?" Mel asked.

Tearloch answered, "The fae and human realms coexist with many others." He cast a dark look at Liam. "Though the chances that one could accidentally slip into another are practically zero."

"There is one realm that all eventually inhabit." Liam shifted uncomfortably.

"Impossible," Cathair snapped.

Mel looked from one fae to the other. "What realm?"

"Spirit," Liam replied.

"What does that mean?" Winnie asked.

Mel voiced her question.

"Dead," Cathair said, his voice laced with outrage. "He's saying Winnie could be dead."

Liam had the good sense to look horrified by the suggestion.

If it weren't so sad, Winnie would have laughed. She wasn't certain of many things anymore, but being alive was one of them.

As the guys kept arguing about what might be going on, Winnie moved a few steps away from the group. Their rising tension was only making her feel worse.

That unsettled, hopeless feeling she had been battling ever since she first crashed into the veil churned in her stomach. She had been fighting the sense of despair, but now it crashed into her.

What if this was a permanent state? What if Cathair could never see her again? What if she never got to enter the veil again?

Mel appeared beside her.

"Hey, we'll figure this out." Mel placed a reassuring arm on her shoulder.

Winnie looked up at her, feeling entirely hopeless. "What if we can't, Mel? What then?"

When Mel responded by pulling Winnie into a big hug, the tears started to fall. Mel wasn't the maternal type. She usually shied away from emotion. If she felt the need to comfort Winnie, then things had to be really bad.

"Is she…all right?"

Winnie looked up to see that Liam had followed them to the edge of the clearing. After extricating herself from Mel's hug, Winnie wiped away the tears. Even though no one but Mel could see them, she couldn't help but try to hide them.

Liam stood so proud. A fierce warrior, afraid of nothing and prepared to take on any challenge. Winnie aspired to be half so brave.

"She's…" Mel cast a sympathetic look Winnie's way, then turned back to Liam. "Worried."

Winnie could start right then. Instead of retreating into despair, she would stand and fight.

"We will solve this," Liam said in that strong, certain tone with which he said everything. With the kind of authority that made Winnie believe what she said. "Whether it takes a day or a decade, we will solve this. You are a member of Clan Moraine. You belong within the veil."

For a career soldier with a hard time relating to others, Liam sure knew how to say the right thing just then. Winnie had never felt more like she belonged. Not just with Cathair, but with the entire fae realm.

She was Moraine now, and the Moraine did not quit.

Winnie straightened her spine as happy tears streaked down her cheeks. She couldn't form words, so she was relieved when Mel said, "She says thank you."

Liam nodded, as if pleased by the response.

"But it won't take a decade," Mel said. "I bet that by the time you wake up tomorrow, this will all feel like a bad dream."

Winnie laughed at the thought. If only it were a dream. If only she could just wake up and find that everything was back to normal. Well, as normal as a life where she could see magical, shapeshifting creatures could be.

If only it were a dream.

"We should take her to the Healing Pools of the Buchalla," Tearloch said in a firm voice that carried across the clearing.

Winnie barely registered his words as a thought tugged at her mind.

"Do you want to kill her?" Liam threw back, returning to the debate. "If she is not magically cursed, the pool will destroy her."

It wasn't possible, she mused as the boys argued. She had only ever dreamed of the veil, of life within the fae realm. Never beyond.

Cathair shook his head. "It is too risky."

"Is this situation not worth the risk?"

"Worth killing her?" Liam barked. "No, of course not."

But she'd never been blocked by the veil, either. She'd never been hidden from fae sight. Not in real life anyway.

There was a first time for everything.

Winnie tugged at Mel's sleeve. "Hey, I have an idea."

When Mel saw the optimistic look in Winnie's eyes, she turned to the rest of the group. "Hey, guys."

When they ignored her, Mel crossed the clearing.

"Listen up—"

"What about Callistra?" Tearloch asked.

"I could never trust a witch," Liam spat. "They are too unpredictable."

Tearloch threw his hands in the air. "She is the sister of my beloved. Callie can be trusted."

"She is a valid option," Cathair argued.

"Hey!" Mel shouted, showing signs of irritation. "Guys!"

"We could call to Morrigan."

"The goddess does not think well of humans."

Winnie watched helplessly as Mel tried over and over to get their attention. They were too so involved in their argument to notice. Finally, when Winnie couldn't stand the bickering any longer, she let out a scream.

"Stop it!"

Her words echoed all around them, bouncing off the trees and reverberating through the clearing.

Everyone froze. Cathair with his arms outstretched, keeping his friends from breaking into a brawl. Liam with his chest forward, inviting a challenge from Tearloch, who stood, pointing an accusatory finger at Liam. Mel with her hands on her hips, watching the guys argue.

For a split-second, Winnie thought she might have actually frozen them. Like maybe her outburst had locked the entire forest into a moment in time. With fae magic, anything was possible.

But then, almost as one, everyone gathered in the clearing

turned to look at her. Not *at* her, really. But in her general direction.

They still didn't see her, but it was like they felt her there.

Cathair was the first to speak. "Winnie?"

"You heard that?" she asked.

When he didn't respond, she turned to Mel who repeated the question.

"Yes," he responded, a relieved smile on his face.

"Me too," Tearloch said.

"As did we all," Liam added.

Winnie let out a huge, relieved laugh. This only confirmed her unlikely suspicion.

"I think I know what's going on," she said. "At least, I hope I do."

Mel frowned in confusion. "You do?"

"Yes." Winnie rushed forward and squeezed her friend in a quick hug. "Just…sit tight. I'll be back as soon as I can."

The last thing she saw was Mel's confused expression as Winnie vanished from the clearing.

SIX

December 21, 8:11 pm

WINNIE BLINKED HER EYES OPEN. Instead of looking up at the darkening forest sky, she saw the cracked ceiling of her bedroom.

She laughed out loud.

"It was all a dream."

Now she remembered. When she got home from school, she decided to take a quick nap so she would be ready for the all-night ball. Instead of waking up, she'd traveled to the veil in her dream. She'd spoken with Mel in her dream.

It wasn't surprising that the others hadn't been able to see her. It was only on the rarest occasions that Cathair could see and interact with her while she was dreaming herself in the fae realm. That Mel could was definitely weird.

But she could examine that another time. Now, hopefully for real, she had a Solstice celebration to attend.

Winnie bounded out of bed, giving Nessa a quick pet

before getting dressed and ready—again—only much faster and with much less care for how she looked.

While she hurried through her routine, she thought about the dream. What had made this dream different? Why had she dreamed herself in the human realm instead of the fae? She thought her powers were restricted to seeing the magic in her dreams. Something had changed.

Either the Solstice magic had affected her abilities, or her powers were growing. She was so relieved to know she still had them that she didn't care which it was. She just wanted to get to the veil as quickly as possible. Her friends were waiting for her.

She rushed downstairs and found her aunt still baking in the kitchen.

"Hey, Aunt Mo," Winnie said.

Her aunt screamed, whirling away from her mixing bowl and sending flower flying everywhere. When she saw Winnie standing in the doorway, she clapped her hand to her chest.

"Winnie, good heavens!" she exclaimed. "I thought you were staying the night?"

"I was," she replied. "I am. It's hard to explain."

Her aunt wiped her hands on her apron. "Try."

"When you saw me before, I wasn't really there."

Maureen frowned. No, that was more than a frown. That was a full on scowl.

"I saw you," she argued. "I spoke with you."

"I was in a dream."

Maureen gestured for her to continue.

"It's never happened like that before," Winnie explained.

"I've only ever dreamed myself in the fae realm. But tonight I dreamed myself here."

"And I could see you?" her aunt asked. "And speak with you? How?"

Winnie shrugged. "Magic."

She didn't have any better explanation than that.

Her aunt seemed to consider the situation for a few long moments. Eventually, she shook her head and waved it off.

"Okay then," she said. "So I take it you need another ride to the forest?"

Winnie flashed her a grateful smile. "Please and thank you."

A few minutes later, they were on their way. Back to the parking lot near the veil. Again.

After the roller coaster she had been through that evening, Winnie was grateful that her aunt didn't ask any more questions. Either Maureen had sensed that, or she had given up on making any sense out of fae magic.

She and Winnie both.

As her aunt pulled into the parking lot, Winnie gave her a quick hug. She grabbed the sweater from the back seat.

"Thanks again," Winnie said as she climbed out of the car. She started for the path, called back over her shoulder, "Happy Solstice!"

She heard her aunt call out, "Happy Solstice!" as she raced down the forest path. By the time she reached the clearing, she was out of breath and overheating despite the cold weather.

"Winnie!" Mel saw her first.

Unable to speak, Winnie waved at her friend and then turned her attention to the rest of the group. Mel saw her before, in the dream. The real test would be whether the others could see her now.

Cathair's beaming smile was the only confirmation she needed.

She raced into his open arms, wrapping her arms around his neck as his came around her waist.

"You can see me?" she whispered. "You can really see me?"

He squeezed her tighter than ever. "I can see you. I can feel you. I can kiss you."

And he did.

She wanted to sob with relief as his lips met hers. Moments later, she felt hands patting her on the back.

"Glad to have you back," Tearloch said. "I wouldn't have actually sent you to the Healing Pools."

"But you would have sent her to the witch?" Liam sneered.

"At least I came up with suggestions," Tearloch threw back.

Winnie grinned as Cathair let out a soft growl at them and then focused his attention on her.

"What happened?" he asked.

Winnie rolled her eyes at herself. "I was in a dream. I wasn't physically here."

"Then why could I see you?" Mel asked.

"I don't know." Winnie shrugged. "No one but Cathair has ever seen me in a dream before."

Liam moved to Mel's side. "She is the daughter of a fae god."

"True," Mel said with the same casual agreement as one conceding that the sky was blue. "Being a demi-goddess does come with perks."

"I don't know about the rest of you fools," Tearloch said in a booming voice, "but I am famished. The Feast of Brighid is calling."

"And a certain princess who is a guest of the palace for the Solstice celebration?" Liam teased.

Tearloch blushed. "Perhaps."

The group started for the veil. Winnie watched as first Tearloch and then Mel and Liam passed through to the fae realm. Cathair kept his arm around her shoulders as they approached.

She hesitated. An icy cold sliver of fear slid down her spine.

"What if—" she began to ask.

"No," Cathair said before she could voice her doubts. "You must have faith. Belief in magic is more powerful than the magic itself."

Winnie nodded, steeled herself, and stepped forward. Straight through the veil.

As she felt the magical sparkle over her, she sighed with relief. She hadn't really doubted. Not really. At least that's what she told herself. But Cathair was right. She had to believe.

He squeezed her close as they continued down the path.

"So, are you ready for your first Solstice celebration?"

She leaned into him as they walked. "You have no idea how ready I am."

SEVEN

December 21, 8:55 pm

WINNIE KNEW she would never again confuse a dream with reality. No matter how many times she had dreamed of the Solstice celebration, nothing could compare to the what it felt like to be there.

From the moment they entered the palace, all of her senses were overwhelmed. The smells of richly spiced foods and fresh-cut pine. The sounds of music and dancing and hundreds of spirited conversations. Bright green ribbons and jewel-colored ballgowns lit up by candlelight. She could feel and taste the magic in the air.

Dreams paled in comparison.

With a hand on the small of her back, Cathair guided her through the entry hall crowded with revelers.

"I'm sorry I made you miss the feast."

"There will be other feasts," he replied. "Besides, I am certain my mother saved some favorites for us to share later."

"Later?" Winnie asked. "Aren't you hungry now?"

"Famished," he replied as they entered the ballroom, "but food can wait. I have been waiting all my life for this moment."

"This moment?"

He swept her down the staircase and into the madness of the dance floor. When they reached the center of the room, he pulled her close, wrapping one arm around her waist and taking her right hand in his left.

"This moment." He moved, guiding them into a flowing waltz. "Dancing with the love of my life at the Solstice celebration."

Winnie sighed and let herself be swept away by the magic.

It was all too perfect. The cheery, classical music. The scent of spice and pine and cranberries. The flickering glow of a thousand candles. The feeling that, even though they were surrounded by a crush of dancers on all sides, they were entirely alone in the world. Just the two of them and a perfect Solstice night.

She couldn't have dreamed it any better.

A MYTHMAS CAROL

A SWEET VENOM STORY

ONE

December 24, 2:16 pm

WHOEVER WROTE that Christmas song about busy city sidewalks must have been talking about San Francisco. With only a few short hours left, swarms of last minute holiday shoppers are everywhere. Bundled up against the afternoon chill and hurrying through the streets like desperate elves. As if getting one more gift will make all the difference.

Good thing none of them can see the catoblepa this monster-hunting girl is tracking down Market Street. His ugly mug would downright ruin their Christmas Eve.

Literally. One whiff of that critter's nasty breath would knock out a city block. If he weren't glamouring as an older Taiwanese gentleman with a dust mask in place, none of these last-minute Santas would be celebrating tonight.

My phone buzzes in my pocket. I check the caller ID.

This is the third call from Grace in the last five minutes.

She's persistent to a fault. If I don't answer soon, she'll send out a search party.

I'm not used to having to report in with a sister—let alone two. Being reunited with my triplets after being separated for the first sixteen years of our lives has been a steep learning curve. I'm glad we're together now, but some days I need some alone time.

Today is one of those days.

The catoblepa ducks into a yarn shop. I'm not sure which is more surprising: that the yarn shop is open on Christmas Eve or that a catoblepa might need knitting needles. Unless he thinks the owner looks like a tasty holiday meal.

In the past, I would have bitten without question, sending the stinky creature back to the dark realm where the gods imprisoned all of the mythological monsters after Medusa's grisly murder. But when my sisters and I reopened the door to Abyssos, we agreed to give beastie-visitors a chance to behave.

One strike and they're out, though.

A quick glance in the window reveals no obvious secondary exit, so I station myself by the door and answer the phone.

"Yeah," I say, keeping one ear trained on the shop, listening for sounds of an attack.

"Gretchen!" Grace exclaims. "Finally!"

"Sorry," I tell her. "I'm hunting."

"The catoblepa?"

"You caught that smell?" I ask, impressed. "You're getting better at identifying them."

"After almost four months of nightly training, I would hope so."

A woman inside the shop makes a strange noise. Adrenaline surges into my bloodstream. My body is beyond ready for a real hunt.

When I look inside, I see the shop owner gleefully applauding the yarn choice the catoblepa has made.

This beastie isn't on the hunt for anything more than a craft project. I'll leave him to his knitting.

A dissatisfied feeling settles into my chest. I'm not sure if it's because I'm itching for a hunt that nine times out of ten leads to a disappointing result or because for the first four years of my hunting career I sent every last monster home, dangerous bad guys or not. I try not to dwell on the past, but the guilt is real.

Pushing away from the door, I start down the sidewalk.

"Did you want something?" I ask.

"Oh, yes," Grace says. "What time are you coming over?"

"Coming over?" I repeat as I turn onto 4th, hoofing it back to where I parked Moira by the Moscone Center. Too bad it's not a long enough walk to burn off any of that unspent adrenaline.

"For Christmas Eve dinner," Grace says with an unspoken duh. "Mom likes to have the turkey on the table by six."

"Turkey?"

"And Tofurky," she adds. "Can you be here by six?"

I shudder at the thought of whatever a Tofurky is. Grace loves that vegetarian cardboard. I can't even bring myself to try it.

"I'm not coming," I tell her.

"What do you mean you're not coming?" she demands.

"Greer is coming. Nick and Milo are coming. The Golden Maiden is coming."

"Isn't Greer Jewish?"

"Exactly. It's a family dinner," Grace pleads. "Even Cassandra is coming. You have to come."

Grace should know by know that I have an inherent aversion to anyone telling me I have to do anything. Ursula was the only person I ever took orders from. She's gone, so I don't take them from anyone now.

And telling me that our biological mother is coming, the woman who gave us up for adoption at birth supposedly to keep us safe from a war we could never escape, isn't exactly a selling point. Grace may be all about welcoming her into our ever-growing family, but my jury's still out.

"Can't," I tell Grace. "Someone has to guard the door."

"That's a stupid excuse."

That kind of admonition sounds more like Greer. No tolerance for sugar-coating is one of the only things I have in common with our overprivileged sister. It's so out of character for Grace that I almost laugh. Almost.

"It's not an excuse," I insist, even though I know it is. "It's the reality of our lives. We don't get time off."

"The city will be safe for a few hours, and you know it."

I do know it. Even though there have been more monster visitors than ever before, they're also mostly harmless. The last big disaster was when a campe dragon decided to visit the Garden Court at the Palace Hotel. Instead of using the main entrance, she came through the ceiling. No casualties, but lots of broken glass.

Just because things have been quiet and relatively harmless

since our battle with Nyx doesn't mean we can let our guard down.

"Look, I'm not coming, okay," I declare. "Just… have fun without me."

There's a long pause, and I can practically feel her disappointment through the phone. I hate making Grace feel bad. I get a not-so-secret thrill out of pushing Greer's buttons, but Grace is the sweet, sensitive triplet. My protective instincts kick into overdrive with her. If I could make sure she never feels another ounce of pain for the rest of her life, I would. I would do almost anything for her.

But I won't do this.

I won't do Christmas.

"If you change your mind," she says, her voice softer than before, "we'll save you some stuffing."

I almost tell her not to bother. But that would be like kicking her while she's down, so I don't say anything.

"Merry Christmas," she says.

I shake off the uncomfortable feeling snaking down my spine.

"Thanks," I tell her and then end the call.

I wish I could say Merry Christmas back, but in my experience, Christmas is anything but merry.

Before I ran away for the last time, the holidays meant extra-drunk foster parents, shouting matches that kept me hiding in my room with the door locked, and lonely nights spent wishing for parents who loved me enough to pretend Santa was real. A wish that never came true.

After I was on my own, the holidays meant hunting down the beasties who thought Christmas dinner meant finding a human to snack on followed by a microwave turkey dinner and, if she was feeling the holiday spirit, occasional praise from Ursula.

Now I don't even have Ursula anymore. I highly doubt she's going to come down from Mt. Olympus to wish me happy holidays. If she did come, it would be to remind me that we may have won the battle against Nyx, but her war isn't over. She'll be back, and I'll be ready.

I can't let my guard down, not for a minute. Greer nearly died last time. I won't let there be a next time.

My sisters can have their perfect family Christmas. There aren't any other descendants of Medusa waiting in line to take my place, so I'm going to do my job. For all of us.

TWO

December 24, 3:37 pm

As the temperature drops, I decide to hit up my favorite coffee shop. A nice steaming hot redeye will keep me warm on my overnight patrol. Plus, The Grindery adds freshly ground nutmeg during the holiday season and, even though I'm not celebrating Christmas, it makes me feel more festive. Or at least less like a grinch.

A girl can pretend, right?

The barista doesn't seem annoyed to be working on a holiday. In fact, she seems extra cheerful.

"Merry Christmas," she says, handing me my drink.

I flash her a half-hearted smile and then head for the door. When I step out into the chill, I wrap my hands around the cup and let the heat warm me. I lift the liquid caffeine to my lips, ready to take a sip when the smell hits me.

A bizarre cross between blueberry jam and fresh fish.

Not exactly the most appetizing aroma. And not one I remember smelling before.

I take a quick chug of my drink, letting the warmth and the caffeine energize me. Then I jump back into Moira and follow the trail of the scent through the crowded city streets. I wind my way toward whatever new mythological creature is making an appearance.

By the time I reach the marina, my coffee is gone, along with my patience, and I'm itching for a fight. I hope this is one bad beastie. My fangs could use the workout.

I scan the area for my quarry.

In the soft glow of sunset, it takes me a minute to spot him. Between all of the mooring posts and sailboat masts, it's hard to pick out a single creature in the mess.

But then I see the flash of a long, winding tail.

"Gotcha," I whisper.

I move into a position where I can get a clear view of the creature at the far end of the east harbor. When I do, I see that it's not a creature at all. Or at least not entirely a creature.

From the waist up he's definitely human, albeit one with blue skin and green hair.

He's sitting on the breakwater, facing out into the Bay, with a fishing pole sticking out in from of him. As I watch, something tugs at the pole. He leans back to reel it in, his lower half kicking up to provide leverage.

His lower half is where the human part ends. Instead of legs, he has a long, fish-like tail. That tail flicks up, splashing a spray of sunset-lit water into the air.

As the water falls back into the Bay like flecks of fire, I

catch sight of the long building on the other side of the marina.

The loft.

Only it's not the loft anymore. Not since Artemis's crew blew it to smithereens as part of Zeus's plan to kill my sisters and me to prevent the war with Nyx. A plan that obviously failed.

The city rebuilt the structure and turned it into some kind of arts center.

I had a lot of memories—both good and bad—in that loft.

It's where Ursula trained me to be the hunter I am today. It's where I took Grace the night we first met, face-to-identical-face in a darkened nightclub. It's where I first felt like I truly belonged. The loft may be gone, but the memories can't be destroyed.

One in particular floats to the top of my mind.

It was my very first Christmas with Ursula. I'd been training with her for a few months, thrilled to finally have a purpose in my life. After doing dozens of hunts with her help and guidance—whether it was sniffing out the beastie in the first place or advising how best to send them back to the abyss —this was the first one I did all on my own.

I'd been standing on the balcony, enjoying the moonlit night while Ursula worked on something in the library.

At first I thought the smell was coming from one of the boats in the marina. It reminded me of ham and I thought someone was having Christmas Eve dinner on the water.

But then the ham smell turned sour, a transformation I had learned meant something from the beastie realm was walking around in ours.

"I think there's a monster in the marina," I told Ursula.

She looked up from the computer. "What does it smell like?"

I described it, and she nodded.

I waited for her to tell me what kind of monster it was or how to hunt it. But her attention went back to the computer.

"Should I go after it?"

She didn't look up. "What do you think?"

It was a test. I knew it was, and I wanted to pass more than anything. I wanted to please her, the only person who had ever thought I was more than just a dirt poor, orphaned runaway.

I went through all the steps she'd taught me. First, I retrieved the hunting supplies from the cupboard in the armory, stuffing anything I thought I might need, anything I'd used on past hunts, in my pockets. I slipped a dagger into the shaft of my boot and secured the kevlar cuffs on my wrists.

Then, without waiting for approval or further instruction, I headed out into the night.

It turned out I could have used a little assistance. When I got to the marina, I found myself face-to-face with a hecatoncheires. A hundred-handed and fifty-headed giant was a little more than I was prepared to handle.

But I wasn't about to ask for help.

The fight wasn't easy. When it was over, the rigging line from a half dozen sailboats had been sacrificed, and one massive yacht ended up at the bottom of the Bay. But I won the day. One swift bite to its dominant hand—number thirty-seven, apparently—and it was en route to its prison realm home.

As he vanished from sight, I glanced up at the loft, panting, exhausted and soaking wet. Ursula stood there, watching.

Had she been there the whole time? Had she been waiting to see if I needed help? Or was she just judging my efforts?

Either way, I'd succeeded. I hoped I made her proud.

When I got back to the loft, she was at the computer again.

I didn't say anything as I headed to the bathroom to take a long, scalding shower to wash away the sour ham and salty fish stink. I emerged twenty minutes later feeling slightly more human again. Or slightly more-than-human again.

Ursula was still in the library, so I headed for the kitchen to get some food.

As I passed by the library door, she called out, "There is something for you. On the counter."

There, at the end of the kitchen counter, was a small box wrapped in plain brown paper. A present? I couldn't remember ever getting a present, especially not a Christmas present. It was a first.

Trying to hide my eagerness, I slowly and carefully peeled away the paper. I removed the lid of the box inside.

There, on a field of black velvet, was a small silver pendant in the shape of a serpent.

Unless my kevlar wrist cuffs counted, I didn't wear jewelry. Partly because I'd never had any. But also because it seemed unnecessary. It would only get in the way.

But this pendant, this serpent that represented my mythological heritage, my ancient, snake-haired ancestor, felt like it belonged around my neck.

When I turned it over, I saw an inscription on the back. A word written in ancient Greek.

ισχύς

I stuck my head in the library door.

"What does it mean?" I asked. "The inscription."

"*Ischys*," she said. "It means strength."

Strength, my mind echoed. I didn't know if it was meant to give me strength or to say that I was already strong. Either way, it was perfect.

"Thank you."

She just nodded.

She didn't need to say anything. We both knew how much it meant.

That had been a good night. Maybe the only good Christmas I've ever had.

My hand instinctively goes to my chest, to the spot where the serpent used to hang. It never left my neck. Not until the night the loft blew up and my sisters and I had to bail into the Bay to avoid getting blown up with it.

Somehow in the process, the necklace had broken free. I didn't even realize it was gone until days later.

I can still feel it. The echo of it.

Shaking off the nostalgia, I head for the half-fish fisherman. No point wasting time on missing something I can't get back.

My first goal is the figure out who—or more accurately *what*—this creature is. I remember Grace going on and on about a merman she read about in the monster files, even before we saw that real-life mermaid on our monster hunt in the Bahamas. Something about a fisherman king who was turned into a demigod. What was his name? Glantus? Glomus? Oh yeah, I remember.

"Catch anything, Glaucus?"

The blue-faced man turns to look at me with a smile. He shakes his head. "Too cold for the fishies."

I take a seat next to him on the wall.

"I wondered if my presence would draw out a huntress," he says.

"Is it a good thing or a bad thing?"

He grins. "It is an honor to meet one of the Key Generation."

"It must be your lucky night," I tell him. "As long as your plans don't involve any hunting of your own."

"You have no reason to hunt me. I always throw them back."

He winks and goes back to his fishing rod.

Great. Another dead-end hunt. My fangs are going to atrophy.

"Then I guess I'll let you enjoy your holiday in peace."

"Shouldn't you be celebrating with your family?" he asks casually. "I hear that the feast of Christmas Eve is a sight to behold."

I wouldn't know. I've never been to one.

Besides, what business is it of this total stranger, demigod or not, to comment on how I spend my holiday?

"Someone's gotta keep the city safe from the likes of you," I say, half teasing and half changing the subject. I hop back down from the wall. "If you see any undesirables out and about, you tell them I'm on the prowl tonight."

Glaucus gives me a mock salute. "Yes, ma'am."

"Have a nice night," I tell him as I walk away.

"Any night fishing," he replies, "is a nice night indeed."

I cast one last look at the building that sits where the loft used to be.

I guess Glaucus feels the same way about fishing as I do about hunting. Any night spent trolling for beasties is a nice night indeed. Certainly better than one spent in an overcrowded apartment, pretending like everything is perfect for a night.

I palm my keys and start back on patrol.

THREE

December 24, 4:04 pm

I'm DRIVING up Fillmore when I catch the next scent of the night. Unlike the last smell, this one is all too familiar. I've experienced it way more times than I ever wanted to. On an almost daily basis.

And as much as I might insist that I don't want to see the source—ever—I steer Moira in the direction of its origin.

As I make my way toward the Bay Bridge overpass, I tell myself that I'm just checking on him. That I just want to make sure he's not causing or getting into any trouble.

But deep down, in a soft place in a corner of my heart that I refuse to admit even exists, part of me just wants to see him. I want to make sure he's okay, that he's staying warm on this increasing chilly night.

If he ever heard me say those things, I would never be able to get rid of him.

The sun is long gone by the time I get to the small, fenced-in area that Sillus and his extensive family call home. During the day, the place is a busy construction and maintenance staging area. I have no idea where most of them go in the daylight hours. Sillus is usually somewhere on my tail, but somehow they all manage to avoid getting caught by the crews who swarm this spot during working hours.

I park far enough away to keep my presence under the radar. The last thing I want is to be accosted by a bunch of furry little monkey creatures.

The afternoon has turned cold enough that I dig out my gloves and pull them on as I walk to the site.

I can hear the celebration from a block away. Dozens of high-pitched voices, singing or arguing or just talking about whatever the heck cercopes have to talk about.

I step up to the chain link fence and stare, in awe, at what's happening within.

A massive bonfire lights up the entire area. It doesn't look so big that the fire department will notice, but the glow it casts spreads far beyond the fence. I can feel the heat of it on my face, and I find myself leaning in to be closer to the warmth.

A small group of Sillus's relatives is in one corner of the lot, playing something that might be called music. They're using instruments I've never seen before, and sound is coming out of them in some kind of rhythmic fashion, but that's where the similarities to music end.

Still, it must sound great to the dozens of other cercopes, because most of them are dancing around the bonfire with wild abandon. It looks like complete and total madness, like tales I've read about Dionysian parties, but they look like they're having fun.

A long table has been set up along one far edge of the lot. It is literally covered end-to-end in plates, bowls, and baskets of food. There is so much bounty there that I think the table might eventually collapse.

One cercopes who looks slightly larger and older than the rest stands next to the bonfire, manning the handle of a giant spit that is roasting something over the open flame—I can't tell what from this distance and, honestly, I probably don't want to know.

A group of young cercopes races along the fence in front of me, one waving what looks like a giant burrito in front of him and the others giving chase.

The scene looks like something from one of those old Hollywood movies that always play on repeat during the holidays. A huge family celebration, full of merriment and mischief. I half expect a cercopes dress as Santa Claus to jump out from behind a dumpster and give out gifts to all the little monkey children.

The craziest thing is that some small part of me wants to join them. I have the urge to slide open the gate and lose myself in the sheer chaos of the party.

Which is possibly the most ridiculous thing I've ever thought. I hate crowds more than I hate holidays and cercopes combined. This party is the Gretchen Sharpe trifecta of things I can't stand.

Besides, I'm sure they don't want me here. They're all having a great time. Well, everyone except for the kid with the burrito. He's been tackled by the others—and several more of their friends—and they are wrestling the burrito from his furry little hands. Everyone else is having the time of their lives.

The last thing they want is a huntress crashing the party.

I have better things to do anyway.

Giving the boisterous celebration one last glance, I turn away from the fence.

"Huntress!"

Sillus's furry little face is so full of optimism and expectation that I can't even pull off the I'm-disgusted-to-see-you look that I usually show him.

I give him a half-hearted smile instead. "Hey, Sillus."

"Huntress come for Christmas?" he half asks half squeals.

I've never really understood why he's so attached to me. From the very start, he's looked at me with the kind of heart eyes that rescue puppies show their owners. I may act like I hate it, but it gives me a fuzzy feeling inside.

Another thing I'll never tell him.

"No, no," I hurry to insist. "I just came by to check on you."

His face melts into an expression of bliss. "Huntress worry about Sillus."

"Yeah," I say, falling back into my normal routine with him. "Worried that you and your family are going to take over the city if I don't keep an eye on you."

Sillus waves off my jaded comment. He's used to them by now. They stopped affecting him a while ago.

"Sillus family no want city," he says with a dismissive laugh. "Only want happy Christmas."

"Good to know."

I nod and start to walk around him, eager to get away before I get pulled into something.

"Where huntress go?"

"I have things to do," I tell him.

"Christmas with sisters?" he asks.

I shake my head. "I'm on duty. I have to patrol."

Before I can turn away and go back to the safety of my car, Sillus lunges forward and grabs my hand.

"No, no, no." He pulls at me, trying—and failing—to drag me toward the gate. "Huntress stay. Huntress no work."

Even if he weren't the size of a small goat, my super-strength would keep him from ever being able to budge me. That doesn't stop him from trying. I feel like a cartoon giant as I lift him into the air and hold him at a distance.

"Someone has to."

Although I say the words to Sillus, I feel like I'm also saying them to myself. Like I'm trying to convince myself that it's true, that I can't abandon my duties for even a night.

I know it's a lie. There are plenty of times when the city is left unguarded. When Grace, Greer, and I are in school. When we get a report of a far-roaming monster and have to *autoport* somewhere else in the world to take care of it. When we went to Abyssos and used the back door to get into Mt. Olympus.

The insistence that I have to work just an excuse. I know that. My sisters know that. Heck, even Sillus knows that.

It's not a lie I'm willing to let go of.

"Besides," I tell him as I set him back on the ground. "Even the thought of being trapped in there with your hundreds of family members gives me a rash. You know I can barely take one of you at a time."

Sillus makes a funny clucking noise, like he thinks my excuse is totally ridiculous.

"Family nice," Sillus says. "Family important."

I glance in again at the merriment. I feel a pang of envy, like maybe I really would like to know how it feels to be surrounded by such a huge and loving family.

But with hope comes the opportunity for hurt. I've had my lifetime fill, thank you very much.

"If no stay here," Sillus says. "You go sisters. Christmas with sisters."

"I told you I can't." I yank my hand from his furry little grip.

He blinks at me several times in that same innocent, pleading way that Grace looks at me when I've disappointed her.

"Okay, okay," Sillus says, recovering his humor. "But you take gift. From me to sisters. To family."

He scurries away before I can tell him no. I wait for him to come back, impatient to be gone but not wanting to be rude. And maybe a little bit curious to see what he considers a gift.

When he returns, he's carrying a package roughly the size of a football, wrapped in newspaper and tied with what looks like a shoelace. It smells like a spice factory.

"Here." He presses it into my hands. "Take."

Sillus and his family don't have much in this world—or any other. The gift means a lot.

A tiny bit of the ice melts around my heart. I lean down and wrap my arm around him in a gentle hug.

"Thank you," I tell him, actually meaning it. I might not be willing to eat what's inside, but I appreciate the gesture.

"Merry Christmas, huntress," he says, squeezing me back.

"Go," I tell him. "Get back to your party."

He nods and then hurries back into the festivities.

As he disappears into the furry crowd, I whisper, "Merry Christmas."

Then, before I lose my mind and follow him into the party, I turn and walk away.

FOUR

December 24, 5:41 pm

I DECIDE to make a stop at home to drop off Sillus's football package, trade my leather jacket for a warmer coat, and get a fresh mug of coffee in my system before going back on the beat.

That plan evaporates as I steer Moira toward the Tenderloin and I catch another scent. I've smelled this one before, too, but it's not one I'm excited to repeat.

The last time I faced an amphisbaena, I got two snake bites—one from each head—before managing to get my own bite in. Their venom is excruciating and long-lasting.

But at least I know I can survive it. Which is more than I can say for any unsuspecting humans that come across its path. There is no presumption of immunity this time. Some creatures are born bad.

I make a sharp right on Montgomery and follow the stench.

My heart rate speeds up as I realize where the smell is coming from. Russian Hill. The neighborhood isn't far from Grace's apartment building.

The hair on the back of my neck stands up as I floor the gas.

The sun has disappeared into the Pacific, and the streets are starting to empty. I guess because normal people are at home, eating dinner with their families, stuffing themselves with turkey, sweet potatoes, and green bean casserole. That makes my job easier and limits the potential damage the two-headed snake can cause.

I break several traffic laws to make it to the source before tragedy strikes. The smell is coming from Helen Wills Park, which isn't a park by any standard definition. It's a true urban park, all basketball and tennis courts and playground equipment. Not a bush or a blade of grass in sight.

There's an open parking spot on Broadway, which is a Christmas miracle in and of itself. I stow Sillus's football in the passenger seat and check my hunting gear.

My mistake last time I battled the amphisbaena was going for the heads first. I need to secure the tail and then deal with the venomous heads one at a time after I've limited the beastie's movement.

With that plan in mind, I grab a coil of airplane cable out of Moira's trunk and sling it over my shoulder. This bad boy isn't getting the better of me tonight.

The park gates are locked up tight, but it doesn't take much effort to hoist myself up over the chain-link fence.

The moment my feet hit the concrete, I know something is off.

First—and I probably should have noted this before jumping into an enclosed area with the venomous monster— there's no serpent tail flicking around. Amphisbaena are huge. This park isn't big enough for them to be hiding entirely from view.

Second, the smell has vanished. Like there's not a trace left in the air. Like I'd imagined the whole thing.

That's never happened before.

Maybe the creature took itself back to Abyssos? I've never seen it happen in my more than four years of hunting, but there's always a first time.

Even if it had, though, the scent would linger. A scent this strong would last a few hours, at least.

Fighting the feeling of unease in my stomach, I decide to take one lap through the small park, just to make sure the big-and-nasty isn't hiding somewhere clever.

I'm making my rounds behind the massive playground structure when I sense movement behind me.

"Good evening, Gretchen."

I spin around and find myself facing one of the last people I ever expected to see again.

The oracle.

The woman with the second sight who first told me I was something more than human. The woman who played a huge —and somewhat controversial—role in our fight with Nyx.

My emotions are definitely mixed here.

Greer tells me she has some weird, ancient name, but to me, she will always be simply *the oracle*.

"You are surprised to see me," she says with a wrinkled smile.

Shouldn't I be? The last time I saw her was during the battle with Nyx. And even then, I didn't get to speak with her. She was solely focused on Greer, the triplet who shares her gift of prophecy. Not even a high five after we won.

She's been a ghost ever since.

"It's been a while," I finally say.

I'm not bitter. Okay, maybe a little. This is the woman who told me what I was, who told me that I wasn't crazy and that there was a reason I saw monsters. And then after the battle she just... vanished.

At least when Ursula left, I got an explanation. She didn't just go off to Mt. Olympus to become a goddess and sit on the council of justice without saying goodbye.

The Oracle smiles in that cryptic way that she has.

"My reasons for not... saying goodbye, as you say," she says, proving that she can still read my mind, "are for another day."

She steps closer to me.

In the faint glow of the street light, I can barely see her. She seems older than the last time. Not that I have any clue how old she is. She might have been around for centuries, for all I know.

"I have drawn you here because I have an important lesson for you. Are you prepared to learn it?"

It's hard not to laugh. She's been MIA for months, and now she shows up on Christmas Eve to teach me a lesson? If it's about how to disappear without a trace, then she definitely nailed it.

I study her for several long seconds, debating whether or not to let her know how mad I am. I know I'm not just angry.

I'm also hurt. And since I'm not ready to unpack that emotion right now, I shove it aside.

"Yeah," I tell her. "Sure."

I feel more than see her smile of approval.

"Do you know that even the gods enjoy days of rest during holidays and festivals?" She turns her face toward the sky as if she's staring up at the gods themselves. "In order to recharge their powers, reset their minds, and renew their duty. They enjoy the rest and spending time their families."

She pauses briefly, turning her pointed gaze back to me.

"Do you not agree that such respites are necessary? Particularly for those with the highest missions?"

Her face is a study of innocent expression. But I understand the piercing gaze, the intensity with which she anticipates my answer. An answer that is supposed to be yes. I'm supposed to say, *Oh of course the gods take rest. Of course they spend time with their families. Obviously I should be doing the same. Duh.*

But I've never liked walking into a trap. Not one with a monster waiting at the end or one laid by words.

I don't play that game.

I give her my best blank stare.

"I know your past haunts you. I understand your resistance." Her head tilts slightly. "I understand the fear that holds you at a distance."

My spine stiffens. That was the wrong thing to say.

She can judge me all she wants. She can shame me for not wanting to spend the holidays with my sisters or for being too devoted to my job. But no one, not even an almighty oracle, questions my courage. What fears I have, do not define me. They do not control me.

"Take no offense," she warns. "This fear is not the kind that sheer bravery alone can overcome." Her smile softens. "It is one that only fades with time. With years spent growing together as a family. With trust. And if you do not conquer this fear, the consequences will be dire for those you care most about."

Something about her warning makes me shiver.

I feel a faint tremor in my voice as I insist, "I have literally no idea what you're talking about."

"Your sisters need you." She shakes her head. "Without you, their future is very bleak indeed."

I snort more loudly than I mean to, covering my unease with disdain. The oracle might know a lot of things, but she's wrong about this. My sisters had great lives before I crashed into them.

"You do not believe me. Come," the Oracle says, stepping closer and holding out her hands, palm up. "Let me show you."

I know she's wrong. She has to be. But that doesn't stop the doubts from swirling around me.

Against my better judgment, I reach out with shaking hands.

The instant our palms touch, the dark, shadowy playground around me is gone. I'm on an equally dark, shadowy street, somewhere else in the city. A quick survey reveals that it's an alley populated by rats and trash cans.

"Where am I?" I ask.

I'm alone in the alley, but her reply comes into my mind.

"Not where," she says. "But when. This is a future."

"*A* future?"

"One of many possible. One in which your sisters no longer have you."

Before I can compute with that means, I hear voices coming from somewhere down the alley. Familiar voices. It sounds like my sisters. Like them, but not. Older maybe.

I make my way toward the voices, cautiously in case my ears are deceiving me. But as I get closer I can see that the two girls are clearly Grace and Greer. They must be at least a few years old older than they are now.

"I told you to dodge left," the older version of Greer says.

She looks like she came straight from a society party. She's wearing an expensive coat and completely impractical heels. Her makeup is immaculate, with her hair twisted up into an intricate bun dotted with sparkly gems.

The softening that I've seen her eyes lately, the fading of the queen bee attitude, is gone. This version of Greer is full on frozen.

She crosses her arms over her chest, radiating the air of superiority that surrounded her when we first met. The superiority that makes me want to punch her in the face. The superiority that had begun to wane in our time together.

She's like an ice sculpture.

Grace, on the other hand, looks completely melted. Broken. There are dark bags under her eyes. She's wearing a worn leather jacket that looks like the one I'm wearing tonight. Only this one has holes worn in the elbows, frayed hems at the wrists, and half the zipper is hanging off the front.

No light shines in her eyes. No smile brightens her face. This is not the Grace I know.

She doesn't respond to Greer's accusation. Just shrugs and looks blankly at the giant crab lying at their feet.

Greer starts laying into her about the hunt. As Grace shrinks more and more into herself. I run to them, wanting to hug Grace close and tell Greer to back off.

But since I'm not really here, my arms go straight through Grace. Neither of them can see me.

I feel a sting in my eyes. Since I'm not used to the sensation, it takes me a minute to realize that it's tears. The thought of my sisters turning into what they used to be—no, into the extreme versions of what they used to be—rips my heart in two. They've both been making so much progress: Grace becoming more and more confident, Greer becoming more and more human.

How could they turn into this?

"What's wrong with them?" I ask the non-present Oracle.

"They are without you," she says. "They do not have your drive to train them. They do not have your forthright attitude to bind them together. Without your courage and inspiration, they are, in a word…"

"Lost," I finish for her.

In a flash, the alley and my sisters are gone, and I'm back on the playground with the oracle.

The oracle's lesson is clear. My sisters and I need each other. I will do whatever it takes to keep them from turning into the worst versions of themselves. Whatever it takes. No exceptions.

"Do not discount the value of family," she says. "Do not discount your value to them."

"No." I shake my head. "I won't."

She smiles and then turns to leave.

I want to thank her for what she's shown me, and for what she gave me with her reading all those years ago.

"Do you want to—"

She lifts a hand to stop my offer. "I have holiday plans," she says. "But thank you for asking."

I didn't actually get to ask. But I guess with an oracle I don't have to.

As she moves off into the shadows, I head for my car. I guess I have plans too.

FIVE

December 24, 6:25 pm

I DON'T RING the buzzer or let anyone know that I'm coming. Partly because I want it to be a surprise. And partly because I want to give myself every last possible chance to back out.

The urge to retreat is overwhelming. This is what the oracle meant about fear.

But as the rickety old elevator climbs to Grace's floor, I know that backing out isn't an option. Not anymore. After what the oracle showed me, I'd have to be as self-centered as Ice Sculpture Greer to walk away.

When the elevator doors open, I only hesitate for a moment before stepping out into the hall. My hand is shaking as I lift it to knock on the door of Grace's apartment.

There is some commotion inside. A few seconds later the door swings open. Greer's face, a perfectly polished version of my own, is looking back at me.

She smiles. "I knew you'd come."

"Did you?" I grumble.

She taps one sparkly gold manicured finger to her temple. "I always know."

I can't help but roll my eyes at the sheer size of her ego. She's been a know-it-all from the start, but now that she has better control of her psychic powers she's practically unbearable.

Knowing that my presence in her life helps keep that ego in check makes me bite back my retort.

"Grace will be really glad you came," she says, dropping the arrogant attitude for once.

It's on the tip of my tongue to say something snarky in response. That's our normal routine. But the ice cold vision of future Greer makes me ask instead, "And what about you?"

She leans back like she's surprised by my question. In a moment of sisterly connection, she nods.

"I'm glad too." Then the moment is over. She turns into the apartment and calls out, "Gretchen's here."

A wave of noise echoes from within, followed by a squeal.

Before I know it I'm being swept into the apartment as Grace pulls me into a tight hug.

"I was so hoping you'd come," she says, not hiding a single ounce of the joy in her voice.

It fills me we something suspiciously like the Christmas spirit to know that I made her happy.

I hug her back. "Just couldn't stay away."

I meant for that to sound teasing, but it came out more sincere. I'm surprised to realize that it was.

Clearly, the oracle's vision of the future has messed with my brain.

"Gretchen, honey." Grace's mom pulls me into an even bigger hug. Now I know where Grace gets its. "It just wasn't going to be the same without you."

"Thanks," I tell her, letting myself enjoy the warm feeling. "Sorry I'm so late."

She leans back and makes a dismissive gesture. "Don't be silly. Family is never late."

"Here." I offer her the paper-wrapped football. "This is from Sillus."

"Oh, he's too sweet." She holds it up to her nose. "This smells wonderful."

"I have no idea what it is," I hurry to tell her. "Who knows what those the little monkeys bake into their Christmas goodies."

Grace's mom beams at me. "I'm sure it's delicious."

I hope she's right.

As she takes it off to the kitchen, I look around at the madness in the apartment. Grace wasn't exaggerating when she said everyone would be here. The place is packed with friends and family, members of the Sisterhood of the Serpent—including Cassandra, who flashes me a small smile but knows enough to keep her distance—and several harmless monsters Grace has adopted since we opened the door. It's more than a little overwhelming.

My flight instinct is urging me to run.

"Hey there, stranger."

I turn and see Nick leaning back against the door, almost as if he knows I'm fighting the urge to flee. We saw each other yesterday, but it feels like longer. I'm trying to take it slow with him, but every time we're together, I find myself falling deeper and deeper.

The mischievous grin on his face tonight is just one of the reasons I love him.

It's certainly not because of his fashion sense. He's wearing what has to be the most hideous Christmas sweater ever to exist on the face of the planet. It is bright green and covered with dozens of little terrifying looking elves wrapping equally terrifying looking packages.

I'm not sure how Christmas presents can look terrifying, but these ones managed to pull it off.

"What," I ask, not hiding my revulsion, "is that?"

"This old thing?" He pulls at the sweater and glances down, as if inspecting it for the first time. "It's a holiday classic."

I step closer to him. "It's hideous."

He shrugs in that nonchalant way he has. "You are entitled to your opinion."

"It's not an opinion. It's a fact. Those elves are the stuff of nightmares."

His eyes twinkle. "I'll protect you."

That doesn't even warrant an eye-roll.

With a devious smile on his face, he takes me by the hand and leads me out of the entryway. With all of the assembled party hanging out in the kitchen and the dining room. Nick leads me into the living room, where Grace's granddad is sound asleep in the overstuffed armchair.

Nick leads me to the couch, to the end furthest from the snoring senior.

I make a show of looking above our heads.

"What are you doing?" he asks.

"Checking for mistletoe." I tell him. "A girl can never be too careful at one of these parties."

His smile twists into a smirk. "It's cute that you think I need mistletoe as an excuse to kiss you."

Before he can make a move, I wrap my hand behind his neck and press my lips to his. I feel him smile against my mouth as we lean into each other.

This—him—makes me feel more at home than anything or anyone else. He feels like Christmas.

"Clearly," he whispers against my lips. "I'm the one who should have been checking for mistletoe."

I smile back. "It's cute that you think I need mistletoe as an excuse to kiss you."

I go in for another kiss, but he jerks back.

"Oh wait, I don't want to forget."

He leans to the side and reaches into his pocket. A moment later he pulls out a small package wrapped in paper that, tragically, matches his sweater.

My heart sinks—not with revulsion, but with guilt.

"I didn't get you anything."

Then again, I didn't get *anyone* anything. This is my first real Christmas after all.

His eyes soften, and he turns serious. "You already gave me everything." He presses the gift into my hand. "Open it."

I smile and shake my head as I tear off the wrapping paper.

Inside, I find a necklace. A familiar serpent pendant hanging from a thin silver cord.

"Is this…?"

It looks identical to the one I lost in the loft bombing. I flip it over. The inscription is there.

ισχύς

Strength.

He shrugs, but I can see the pride lurking under the facade of nonchalance.

"A sea daemon owed me a favor." He takes the necklace from me and secures it around my neck. "Didn't take them long to find it on the Bay floor."

"Thank you," I tell him, in the most heartfelt way I can. "This is one of the nicest things anyone has ever done for me."

When he tries to shrug it off again, I kiss him.

As Christmas carols drift in from the kitchen, along with the warm sounds of conversations and dinner preparations, I realize this is how Christmas is supposed to be. Surrounded by friends and family, in the arms of the boy I love, celebrating the season by both giving and receiving joy.

Maybe, just maybe, there is something magical about Christmas after all.

SNOW FALLING ON SERFOPOULA

AN OH. MY. GODS. STORY

ONE

December 28, 8:25 AM

WHAT ADARA SPENCER loved most about doing yoga on the beach was how she could pretend to be somewhere else. Like she wasn't stuck on this tiny Greek island, trapped at this school, and surrounded by people who couldn't possibly understand what she was going through.

On the beach, she could just float away.

She folded forward, grabbing her ankles to stretch out her lower back.

Her beach of choice had an added bonus. It was at the far end of the island and required a steep climb down to reach the perfect white sands. It was hard to find and even harder to access unless someone came the long way around the island.

Which meant she had never once seen another living soul.

That was exactly what she needed.

Since her problem was feeling too alone in the world, she would have thought that actually being alone would only make her feel worse. But for some reason, it made her feel more connected. Connected to the earth. Connected to the ocean. Connected to her mother on Mt. Olympus, her father in Hong Kong, and the rest of the world, wherever they were.

Apparently it was possible to feel overwhelming loneliness and at the same time to like being alone.

Sinking into her practice, she pushed those thoughts about aloneness and loneliness away as she let herself focus on her body, on her breath. She walked her hands forward into a downward dog as she began her sun salutations.

She had just stretched her chest high into upward facing dog when she heard the first crunch of footsteps.

Her muscles immediately tensed up. The footsteps came from farther down the beach, from someone who was taking the long trek around the island.

Adara closed her eyes and tried to ignore the sounds. She would not let the intruder destroy her sense of peace. She exhaled and moved into downward facing dog, refocusing her attention on her breathing.

The footsteps grew louder with her every breath.

She started counting. In, one. Out, two. In, three. Out—

"Adara?"

In a flash, her inner peace shattered into a million shards. Every muscle in her body tensed into stone. Of all the people she did not want to see on her private beach, this one was at the top of the very long list.

Adara pushed herself up to a standing position, abandoning her practice. There was no coming back from that interruption. She would get no mental peace now.

"Hi Phoebe," she said, not disguising her annoyance.

That tone used to keep Phoebe at bay. Adara preferred it that way. But now Phoebe seemed to think they were friends.

Phoebe jogged up the beach and stopped right in front of Adara's mat.

"I hope I'm not interrupting anything."

Adara refused to give Phoebe the satisfaction of admitting that she had. "Of course not."

"Are you doing yoga?"

Adara looked pointedly down at the mat she *visiomutated* from sand before each practice, choosing a different color and pattern each day to keep things fresh. Today's design consisted of a pale blue mat covered in darker blue paisley.

It had been very calming.

She glanced back at Phoebe with arched an eyebrow. "Is that a rhetorical question?"

Phoebe huffed out an awkward laugh. "Yeah, I guess so."

A long silence stretched between them. Finally, Phoebe's expression turned serious.

Adara braced herself.

"So," Phoebe said, cautiously, "how are you…?"

Adara didn't reply. She just stared at her blankly.

If that wasn't a clear message that she wasn't in the mood to talk, Adara didn't know what was.

Not that Phoebe took the hint.

"I mean, this is your first winter holiday without your—"

"For the love of Zeus, Phoebe, my mother isn't dead," Adara snapped before the other girl could say more.

"I know," Phoebe said, undeterred, "but she's gone just the same."

Adara's patience ran out the instant that look of pity started to appear in Phoebe's eyes.

"I'm fine." Adara forced her muscles to relax. "Everything is fine."

If there was one thing she hated more than the fact that her mother had left to serve Apollo for the next twenty-five years, it was the fact the Phoebe knew about it.

The only silver lining was that Phoebe hadn't told any of her misfit friends. Few on the island knew. Adara had told Griffin when the weight of everything became too much to bear alone. She told Phoebe when her relationship with Griffin was at stake. Headmaster Petrolas knew because somehow he knew everything.

They were the only three who knew what was going on. Adara preferred it that way.

She didn't want anyone's pity.

"Do you want to come over for dinner?" Phoebe asked. "Hesper is making a huge Haloa feast. With Stella back at Oxford and Griffin on his quest, it's way more than we can possibly eat."

Adara stifled a groan. She and Phoebe had never gotten along, which was how she preferred it.

But ever since Phoebe learned the truth, she acted like there was something that bonded them together. Phoebe was always asking Adara how she was, if she needed anything, if she wanted to come over for family dinner.

Even if Phoebe meant well, the constant checking in and invitations only put a spotlight on how much was wrong in Adara's life.

"I have plans," she said, without explanation.

Plans that involved takeaway from the school cafeteria and some quality reading time.

She stepped back to the top of the mat, effectively dismissing Phoebe and hoping the girl took a hint for once.

She did.

"I'll let you get back to your yoga," Phoebe said.

She stood there as if waiting for a response.

She would be waiting a long time.

Adara restarted her sun salutations. Eventually, Phoebe turned and continued her run down the beach. Adara hoped a few extra sequences would get her back to zen.

TWO

December 28, 9:42 AM

As Adara climbed back up the cliff path an hour later, she felt frustrated. After Phoebe's disruption, she had never fully gotten back to her practice. Every time she drew in a deep breath, she saw the pity in Phoebe's eyes, which only made her angry. How dare Phoebe pity her? How dare *anyone* pity her? She was the envy of the school. She pitied *them*.

No wonder she couldn't get back to her inner peace.

The anxious and angry energy still buzzed through her body. Maybe a long, hot shower would erase it all.

But as she reached the fork in the path back toward campus, she didn't turn off in the direction of her dorm. It wasn't a conscious decision. Her feet moved on instinct. She found herself crossing through campus and toward the village beyond.

A few minutes later she was climbing the steps of the pantheon temple.

Though most temples catered to individual gods, the pantheon temple was dedicated to all. It granted all gods access to their descendants, and their descendants access to them.

Adara hadn't visited the temple recently. She was too angry at the gods to speak to them. She blamed them for stealing her mother away, even though she knew in her heart it was her mother's choice. She raged at them for letting her father abandon her too, throwing himself into his work to the exclusion of all else. She couldn't even grieve with him because he was too busy making business deals to take her calls.

The anger hadn't gone away in the months since her mother left. In fact, it was worse than ever. Bad enough that Adara knew she probably shouldn't talk to the gods. Bad enough that she felt she had to.

The door was open, and after she slipped inside, she closed it behind her. The interior glowed with the light of a dozen candlelit fixtures hanging from the ceiling. In the flickering light, she could make out the murals that lined the temple walls.

Every deity in the pantheon populated the temple murals. Some were difficult to find, especially the demigods. The Olympians were all in the foreground, in positions of prominence. The benefits of power, she supposed.

Apollo and Aphrodite occupied the same wall, separated by Hera, Hermes, a few minor deities, and several nymphs.

Adara crossed to Apollo first.

As much as she wanted to rail at Apollo, to shout and scream at him for stealing her mother away, she knew that yelling at the gods always backfired. The male gods especially had volatile tempers.

She moved on to the painting of beautiful Aphrodite.

Adara's godly ancestor lay reclined, her torso resting in the lap of Dione. It angered Adara to see Aphrodite cradled in her mother's lap when Adara was denied the same pleasure.

Despite all the thoughts racing through her mind, Adara didn't know what she wanted to say. Nothing maybe. Maybe she would just stand there, staring at the goddess and mentally raging. Mentally begging for help.

As she approached the painting, the weight of her grief became too much to bear. She fell to her knees before the mural.

With her eyes lowered, her hands on her thighs, the words began to tumble out.

"I miss her," she said simply. "It's only been a few months, and I miss her more every day."

She looked up at the mural. She shouldn't expect the goddess to move, or to show her presence in any way, but still Adara hoped. Shouldn't Aphrodite care that one of her descendants was in distress?

"How am I supposed to make it twenty-five years? I've barely made it twenty-five weeks."

The painting remained still. Lifeless.

"Why did you let her become Apollo's handmaiden?" Adara demanded, as if the goddess of love could have prevented everything. "Why didn't you stop her?"

Adara stared into the goddess's eyes, willing her to appear. She stared so long and hard that her mind started to believe that the painting moved.

A noise rustled behind her. In a flash, she jumped to her feet and spun around, her heart pounding as she expected to see Aphrodite standing behind her.

But the temple remained eerily empty. Adara was alone. As always.

She shoved aside her melancholy thoughts. What was the point of dwelling on things she couldn't change? No one, not even Aphrodite, could help her. She had to help herself. She had to find a way to get past this. Without her goddess's help.

But not today. Today Adara was too angry to move on.

Maybe tomorrow would be better, she told herself as she headed for the door. Maybe tomorrow she could begin to heal.

THREE

December 29, 7:53 AM

ADARA HADN'T BOTHERED to set an alarm.

It still seemed early when she woke up. The sunlight filtering in through her dorm window seemed hazy, as if it were passing through a fog.

Then again, it was the heart of winter. Mornings began later and days ended sooner.

A quick check of her clock revealed that it was later than she thought.

She lay on her bed for a long time staring at the ceiling. She had lived in the same dorm room for the last four years, ever since she moved into the upper school dorm. It was more her home than any she had ever occupied at her parents' house. She knew every crack and stain and texture in the ceiling by heart.

Recently, she had spent even more time staring at the plaster ceiling.

After a few minutes of mentally debating whether to roll over and go back to sleep, Adara sat up in bed. She was surprised to realize that she actually felt a little better. Like maybe, for the first time in a very long time, she was looking forward to the day.

She was not so naive as to believe that anything in her life had changed. There were no signs that the goddess had visited her in the night. The countdown app on her phone still read twenty-four years, five months, nineteen days. Her mother was still gone, and Adara was still alone.

The change was entirely on the inside. An attitude shift. The time for moping was over. It was time to start living again.

Adara climbed out of bed and went down the hall to the bathroom. A few minutes later she returned, with her face washed, her teeth brushed, and ready to take on the day.

She didn't have a plan. She only knew that she would start with a centering yoga practice. Then she would figure it out.

She changed into her yoga clothes and then crossed over to the window. The room could use a little more light.

But as she drew open the curtains, her heart sank.

The view from her window looked out over the campus quad. Where yesterday there had been a field of green grass, today all traces of green were gone. The entire campus was covered in a dusting of white powder.

Serfopoula never got snow. Not in the dozen years that she had been attending school here. Not, as far as she knew, in the entire fifteen-hundred-year inhabited history of the island. And yet, despite centuries of precedent, a thin layer a fluffy white covered every surface that she could see.

That shouldn't have made her sad, but it did.

Others might rejoice at the promise of a white holiday. Christmas was over, but the Haloa festival of Poseidon was still in full swing. She was sure that many on the island would romanticize the snow. For Adara, it only made her think of last year's winter break. When her world began to fall apart.

Her parents had surprised her with a skiing holiday. Two weeks spent in the Swiss Alps, racing down the slopes all day and sipping hot cocoa in front of the massive fireplace at night.

Everything had been perfect. It was the most blissful vacation of her life.

Then, after they got home, her mother announced her plans to become a handmaiden to Apollo. It was as if the entire vacation had been a lie. A bribe to make the horrible truth strike a softer blow.

Now the sight of snow made her think of that time. Not of the blissful mountain holiday, but of the life-changing announcement that came after.

FOUR

December 29, 8:22 AM

Adara yanked the curtains closed. Any sense that today was going to be better than yesterday—or better than any day since her mother shared her fateful news—was gone. Buried under a fine layer of snow.

She crossed to the bed and climbed back in. She had no plans. She had spent every day of winter break so far in the library, getting lost in the stacks and stacks of stories of lives that weren't hers. Trying to avoid the questioning gaze of Ms. Philipoulos, the Academy's librarian.

Today, she only wanted to hide in bed and start over tomorrow.

As she pulled the covers over her head, she fought the tears. For the first time in her life, she wished she was someone else. She wished she could dive into one of the stories that filled the library's stacks and live there.

She wanted any life but her own.

Knock, knock, knock.

Adara startled at the sharp noise. Almost the entire campus had gone home for break. Most of her friends were off on family vacations, shopping the boutiques of Paris, scuba diving in Thailand, or having some other exotic experience. Only a few students remained on the island.

As she reached for the door handle, she had a bad feeling she knew who it was. Not someone she wanted to see.

She wished she could use her *psychospection* to confirm her visitor's identity, but after an incident during back to school week, Headmaster Petrolas had restricted all powers usage in the dorms. Sneaking a peek would earn her a severe detention.

She could choose not to answer. Could bury herself under the covers and pretend to be gone.

There were two problems with that plan.

First, Phoebe wouldn't leave. That girl was persistent beyond sense. If she had even an inkling of a thought that Adara was inside, Phoebe would keep knocking until it drove everyone on the island insane.

And second, some teeny-tiny, she-would-never-admit-it-existed-under-pain-of-death part of Adara actually wanted to see Phoebe. She didn't know why. Maybe she was so desperate for companionship that any companionship would do. Or maybe she wanted to replace the emptiness that filled her with another emotion. One like anger, annoyance, or frustration—sensations that usually accompanied spending time with Phoebe.

Either way, she dragged herself back out of bed and reached for the handle.

With an annoyed smirk in place, Adara opened the door,

expecting to see Phoebe standing there.

Oh, Phoebe was there. But so was her step-sister Stella, who happened to be one of Adara's favorite people, and Phoebe's best friend Nicole, who happened to be one of Adara's *least* favorite people.

"This was not my idea," Nicole said immediately.

Adara ignored her.

"I didn't know you were home," she said to Stella.

"I *autoported* back for Haloa," she explained. "I'm glad I did."

The hair on the back of Adara's neck stood up. There was an expression suspiciously like pity on Stella's face. A quick glance at Nicole showed the same expression.

Adara turned on Phoebe. "You told them."

She held up her hands in surrender.

"I didn't say a word, I swear."

"Actually," Stella said, crossing her arms over her chest, "*I* told them."

Adara frowned. If Phoebe didn't tell Stella, how had she found out?

"I was in the temple yesterday," Stella explained. "I heard your plea to Aphrodite."

A flood of emotions washed through her. Shame for being so angry at her mother and the gods over what was supposed to be a great family honor. Embarrassment for getting caught keeping it a secret from one of her best friends. And, strangely, relief.

It felt good to know the truth was out, that she didn't have to hide it anymore.

Adara felt all of the fight drain out of her. "I didn't want anyone to know."

"When Stella told me what she overheard," Phoebe explained, "she didn't know Nicole was hiding behind the door."

"Not hiding," Nicole hurried to explain. "Just not in the mood to face down the queen bee."

Stella rolled her eyes at Nicole.

"I am sorry," she said to Adara. "But I'm also not sorry. You shouldn't go through this alone."

Which was exactly why Adara didn't want anyone to know. Because she *did* want to go through it alone. She wanted to rage and grieve and despair all by herself. Without anyone— friend or foe—to judge.

Just because she was relieved to have the secret out, didn't mean she wanted to throw a pity party.

"I appreciate the concern," she began, her body inching back into the room, preparing to close the door in their faces. "But I'm really busy."

Nicole snorted at the blatant lie.

"Fine, I'm not busy at all," Adara countered. "I just want to be alone."

"That's why we're here," Phoebe said.

That made no sense. Then again, Phoebe often made no sense.

"We don't think you should be alone," she continued. "Even if you think you want to be, you really shouldn't."

That brought the anger right back up to the surface.

Adara was done with people dictating her life. Done with people making choices for her. Done with people making choices that completely upended her life.

She made her own choices.

"Thanks for telling what I should or shouldn't want. But I don't need anyone telling me what to do."

She started to close the door. Before she could get it all the way shut, a heavy black boot jammed itself into the frame.

Adara was so startled that she didn't stop Nicole from pushing the door back open.

"Look, I get it," Nicole said. "I've been there. I did the whole keep-your-distance thing. Got the t-shirt to prove it. And you know what?"

Adara didn't think the question required an actual answer.

She gave up the fight and retreated to her bed. She didn't care anymore if the trio came in. If she hid under the covers and pulled the pillow over her head, maybe she could drown them out.

"It didn't help. I thought I could handle all my anger on my own, but I couldn't. I took friends like these—" Nicole gestured and Phoebe and Stella, and then did a double-take smirk at Stella. "Well, maybe not like *her*."

Stella just smirked back.

Nicole continued, "It took my friends to make me realize how much my anger was hurting me." She stepped closer and sat on the bed. Adara instinctively leaned away. "They made it better," she said earnestly. "You and I are never going to be besties. But these two actually care about you. Let them help."

"I..." Adara opened her mouth to say... something, but she couldn't figure out what. No words came out.

"We're not talking about a kumbaya therapy session," Nicole said.

"You don't even have to talk to anyone if you don't want to," Stella added.

Phoebe jumped in, "We're going to deliver Haloa gifts. We thought it would be fun for us to do it together."

Adara studied the three girls in her room. They were so very different—from her and from each other. Nicole looked irritated—then again, she always looked irritated. Phoebe looked expectant, hopeful even. Adara had no problem dashing those hopes.

It was Stella's look that finally broke her. Stella looked worried.

The last thing Adara wanted was to worry her friends. That was one of the reasons she'd wanted to keep it a secret. Not because she didn't want their pity, but because she didn't want to cause them any pain. She wanted to protect them from her sadness.

But now the secret was out. Whether Adara liked it or not, her friend was worried about her.

She had to remedy that.

She surprised all of them—herself most of all—by saying, "Okay."

"Really?" Phoebe squealed.

Nicole patted her on the shoulder. "Good girl."

Stella just nodded, a small relieved smile on her face.

Adara suddenly felt a little better. Seeing that relief in Stella's eyes made her feel less broken. She had done that. Her small action—one little word of agreement—had brought a measure of relief to her friend. A measure of joy.

That made the prospect of enduring an entire day with Phoebe and Nicole more bearable.

FIVE

December 29, 9:06 AM

ADARA HADN'T BEEN to the village bakery since long before she and Griffin broke up. Unlike some long-distance runners she could name—*cough* Phoebe *cough*—Adara didn't have the metabolism of a hummingbird. If she wanted to keep in shape for track season, she had to steer clear of the carbs and sweets.

The bakery was a temptation she found hard to resist.

The instant Adara walked through the door, she regretted having stayed away. The delightful smell of fresh-baked bread, rising honey puffs, and other sweet holiday treats instantly made her mood better. She couldn't indulge often if she wanted to stay competitive in her racing, but she made a mental note to come in occasionally for a treat.

"Adara!" Aunt Lilika came out of the back room, her apron dusted with cinnamon and flour.

Griffin's aunt was no relation to Adara, but over the years they had become close. Adara had to admit that the breakup was another reason she'd stayed away. Even though she and Griffin were still friends, it felt weird to see his aunt, the woman who had raised him in his parents' absence.

Lilika rushed around the counter and pulled Adara and a soft, warm hug. The kind of hug her mother used to give her.

Adara sank into the warmth and the smell of just-baked gingerbread. "Hi, Aunt Lili. I've missed you," she whispered.

Lilika whispered, "And I you."

When the round-cheeked woman leaned back, Adara saw the sadness in her eyes. She knew it wasn't just about Adara. Ever since receiving the quest that would give him a chance to bring his parents back, Griffin had been gone from home almost as much as he was there. Adara knew he'd left as soon as winter finals were over and hadn't returned.

He couldn't tell them the details of his quest, but they all knew it had to be dangerous. Olympian quests always were.

Lili must have been very worried about him.

Adara felt worse for not coming by. She amended her mental note to include visiting as often as possible. Even if she didn't want a treat, she wanted to see Lili.

"I understand why you did not come," the descendant of Hestia told her. "Do not feel bad."

"I—" Adara started to deny it, but the lie would hurt them both. "I won't," she promised. "And I won't stay away anymore, either."

Lili smiled, but her smile fell slightly. "Is something amiss?" she asks. "There is a sadness in your eyes."

"I—" She glanced at Phoebe and Nicole, who were surveying the treats in the bakery display case. Stella had gone to fetch the candles for the Haloa gifts.

It wasn't as if Phoebe and Nicole didn't already know. And if they knew, it would only be a matter of time before the entire school found out. The entire island after that.

Adara felt closer to Lili than any of them. She would rather tell Lili herself.

Adara let out a deep sigh and quickly explained the situation. She confided in Lili, sharing details not even Griffin knew. The pain, the betrayal, the sense of responsibility to act like everything was fine. It all came out.

When she was done, Lili placed a warm palm on each of Adara's cheeks. "I know this is hard for you," she said in a soft voice. "But I also know that this is a great honor. And for one as giving as your mother, I can imagine that such a life of service is the greatest pleasure."

Adara nodded, but in truth, she didn't understand. Why would her mother give up her home, her family, her entire life to serve Apollo? Sure, it didn't entail the kind of wait-on-him-hand-and-foot service that handmaidens used to perform. Modern handmaidens supported the various charities and causes supported by the god of art, music, and light.

But still, to abandon your entire life for that? Adara didn't understand. She couldn't.

The bell over the door jingled.

"I've got the candles." Stella held up a large basket. She pulled back the cloth to show the stacks of creamy white pillars underneath.

"Oh, are you girls here for the Haloa baskets?" Lili asked.

"Yes," Adara replied somewhat reluctantly, still not entirely on board with the plan, "we are."

Phoebe practically bounced with excitement. "Of all the

new Greek holidays we celebrated last year, Haloa was my favorite."

"That's because you ate the leftover *kourabiedes*," Nicole snarked.

"Not true!" Phoebe cried. "I liked giving out the gifts. I like the whole idea of giving out food and light during the darkest time of year. It's—I don't know…."

She waved her hands like she was reaching for the words.

"Hopeful?" Stella suggested.

Phoebe grinned at her stepsister. "Exactly. Creating light in darkness."

"Such a beautiful way to put it." Lili beamed. "Let me go get the treats."

She went into the back room and re-emerged moments later laden with four heavy-looking baskets. Adara and Phoebe rushed to take them from her.

"I'm afraid I may have gone overboard this year," she said with an embarrassed smile. "But when so many go without, I can't help but share my plentiful bounty."

Adara's stomach grumbled at the delicious smell of Lili's fresh-baked goodies.

"This is wonderful," Stella said. "I am sure the recipients will be very grateful."

"Oh, I almost forgot." Lili ducked behind the counter. When she stood back up, she held a stack of woolen blankets in various colors and patterns. "Because this winter is forecast to be unusually cold, I have been collecting these."

The mention of the cold reminded Adara of the layer of snow that had dusted campus that morning. Only now the snow was gone. On the walk up to the village, she hadn't seen a single flake.

How strange.

"There are not enough for every house," Lili said, handing the stack of blankets to Nicole. "But if you see a house in deepest need…"

"We'll make sure those who need warmth receive them," Stella assured her.

Lili wouldn't let them leave without drinking warm mugs of cider and eating olive rolls, fresh from the oven. Once they had warm hearts and full bellies, they started out into the village with their loads of gifts.

"The Poseidon Alliance gathered enough candles for every house in the village," Stella explained as they walked up the street. "That way no family will feel singled out as one in need."

Phoebe said, "That's great."

"It also means we have to visit literally every house in the village," Nicole replied.

Adara adjusted the grip on her load, a basket full of *koura-biedes* and another of *kariokes*. They were a bit heavy, so she used a little *telekinesis* to lighten the load.

Nicole shifted the stack of blankets in her arms, as if the weight were too much. As if she couldn't wield the same power Adara had just used. She just liked to complain.

Despite the gruff tone and protestations, Adara had a feeling that Nicole was mostly show. Somewhere inside, beneath the thick eyeliner, studded bracelets, and ever-present scowl, there was a soft heart. If Nicole didn't believe in the cause, she wouldn't be there.

It could have been a headmaster-mandated punishment, Adara supposed. But she didn't think so. Nicole cared, whether she wanted to show it or not.

"It may take all day," Phoebe said, clearly taking her friend's complaints in stride. "But think of all the people we will help. Think of how many holidays we will make better."

That seemed to quiet Nicole down. She didn't complain again as the group walked up to the first home and Stella knocked on the door.

SIX

December 29, 4:19 PM

Adara had lost count of how many homes they'd visited.

Door after door, family after family.

The village wasn't that big, but there were dozens of families of all sizes, from one to twenty. All with either some connection to the Academy or to the businesses that support the gods' school.

Some were obviously grateful, thanking them profusely and inviting them inside to share the treats. Others tried to hide embarrassment, quickly taking the offering and ducking back inside. A small minority seemed inconvenienced. As if getting up to answer the door to receive the Haloa gifts wasn't worth their effort.

One grumpy older gentleman had even shut the door in their faces. But Phoebe had carefully wrapped a pair of olive rolls and a candle inside a blanket and left them on his doorstep. By the time they re-emerged from the next home, his bundle was gone.

At every stop, Adara felt more useless. She merely stood to the rear, holding the baskets of cookies, while the others spoke to the families.

Stella was the obvious leader. Many of the village residents knew her since her father was the school's headmaster. Plus, she had lived on Serfopoula her entire life.

Stella spoke easily with everyone they encountered, no matter their background. The perfect hostess.

Phoebe seemed to enjoy talking with the villagers as well. Most of them had heard of her, the daughter of American football star Nicholas Castro and unexpected descendant of Nike. She told them stories of her father's sports career, and they asked about the school's chances in the next Pythian Games.

All the while, Adara and Nicole hung at the back of the group, only stepping forward when Stella or Phoebe needed something from them. They might as well have been pack mules.

Adara just couldn't think of anything to say. And so she kept silent.

As the walked up to the very last house, Adara was relieved that the ordeal would finally be over. Whatever she thought she was going to get out of the experience—or what her friends thought she would get—it was feeling like a big fat zero.

She supposed that, if nothing else, she had carried her weight in cookies. That had to count for something.

As she stood at the base of the steps, waiting for someone

to answer Stella's knock, Adara studied the house. It was not as run down as some they had visited, but it was past due for a coat of paint. The white walls were dull and dirty, and the bright blue trim was chipping in places. Still, it had a cheerful feeling. There was an evergreen wreath on the door, and warm light glowed from behind the curtains.

Movement in the windows to the right of the front door drew Adara's attention. Shifting her gaze, she was surprised to see two tiny faces staring out at her through the glass.

The two girls couldn't have been more than six or seven, all round cheeks, dark curls, and big eyes. They had their noses pressed to the glass. The window fogged with their every breath.

Adara couldn't help but smile at them.

The front door opened and the tiny faces disappeared.

A middle-aged woman welcomed them into the house, into the dining room just to the left of the entrance. Adara recognized the woman from the school kitchen. She was ashamed to admit she didn't remember her name.

She did remember the woman made some of the best food Adara had ever eaten.

"It is so good to see you, Eugenia," Stella said, embracing the woman in a warm hug. "Your *spanakopita* is one thing I miss most at Oxford."

Eugenia. That was it. She would not forget again.

Adara heard a tiny giggle behind her. She turned, searching for the source, and saw the two girls from the window now watching her from the living room.

The bright, smiling faces called to her.

A quick glance at the group confirmed that they were fully

engrossed in conversation with Eugenia. They wouldn't notice if she slipped away.

She crossed the entry hall, knelt down to be at eye level, and set her baskets next to her on the floor.

"Hi there," she said to the two girls. "My name is Adara. What's yours?"

"I'm Cassia," the slightly taller and obviously bolder one said. "I'm seven."

"Nice to meet you." Adara reached out and shook the little girl's hand. "And what's your name?"

The shyer girl moved slightly behind her sister. "I'm Cora."

"Do you girls like *kariokes* and *kourabiedes*?" she asked. "I happen to have quite a few left, and you are the last house we're visiting."

Their eyes lit up as they nodded eagerly. When Adara drew back the cloths on her baskets, both girls rushed forward and peered inside. They took several seconds to choose, inspecting all of the leftover cookies in each before deciding which ones to pick.

"What do you say?" Eugenia said, right at Adara's shoulder.

"Thank you," both girls said in unison before hurrying over to the couch to eat their treats.

Adara felt like she'd been caught sneaking off to meet a boy. It was a ridiculous thought. But she pushed to her feet and brushed off her knees anyway.

"They're very well behaved," Adara said.

"I'm doing my best," Eugenia replied. "Since they lost their mother…."

Her voice faded, like she couldn't finish. Adara looked at Eugenia.

"My sister," she explained. "She and her husband were in a car accident last summer."

Eugenia broke off, unable to finish through the tears. Adara stepped forward and wrapped her arms instinctively around the sobbing woman's shoulders.

There were no words. Nothing could make it better. And so Adara just held her. They held each other.

Adara felt her own eyes fill with tears. For the first time in almost a year, the tears came not for herself and her situation, but for the pain of someone else.

Eugenia was staying strong in the face of enormous grief, putting her own sorrows aside to raise her sister's children. She was a testament to selflessness.

Adara felt ashamed. Since her mother left, she had been feeling nothing but self-pity. Yes, her mother would be gone for a quarter century. But she wasn't gone forever. She would be back.

Compared to true loss, hers was only a temporary sadness.

In an instant, her self-pity evaporated. It took seeing real grief to understand how false and fleeting hers was.

"I'm so sorry," she whispered. Sorry for Eugenia's loss. Sorry for her months of self-pity. Sorry that world could deal such pain on two innocent little girls.

Eugenia hugged her tighter.

"Would you mind," Adara asked, "if I played with them for a while?"

Eugenia leaned back, wiping at the tears on her cheeks. "I'm sure they would love that."

Adara's companions stepped into the hall.

"I don't know about you girls," Phoebe said, looking at Stella and Nicole, "but it's been a really long time since I played Go Fish."

Everyone quickly agreed.

Adara had never head of the game, but Phoebe promised to explain the rules. Minutes later, they were all gathered around the dining table, cards dealt and ready to lay.

As the afternoon wore on, the girls' laughter filled the air, and it was as if they lifted the weight of world a little with every giggle. Replacing sadness with joy. Soon they were all laughing. Even Nicole.

As Adara looked around the table at her friends—yes, she would have to admit she now considered even Phoebe and Nicole her friends—at Eugenia, and the young girls who faced loss too soon, she began to understand why her mother chose to serve. In a flash, as if the god of knowledge himself had formed the thoughts in her mind, it all made sense. To make others feel better, to give her friend a sense of relief, to give joy to a child for even the space of an afternoon, it made *her* feel better. It made her feel joy.

By giving, she received.

That was the true lesson of Haloa. Not just hope and light and gifts. The giving was the gift.

Adara knew that if she was given a chance to feel this way every day for the next twenty-five years, as her mother had been given, she might choose that path as well.

She might not forgive her mother yet—maybe that was something she could never do—but at least she understood.

And with understanding came to means to move on, the means to heal.

Maybe that wasn't what Stella, Phoebe, and Nicole had in mind when they knocked on her door that morning. But she knew that someday she would have to thank them.

That was a Haloa gift worth more than any other.

SEVEN

December 29, 8:47 PM

THE BEACH BONFIRE was the highlight of the Haloa festival. Everyone on the island, from the Academy students and faculty to the residents of the village attends. There was a great feast presented by the Hearth Goddess Club, games and contests for kids and the kids-at-heart, and of course the great bonfire dedicated to Poseidon.

Adara wasn't entirely sure why the sea god needed a bonfire to celebrate his powers, but it was tradition.

Even when used to go home for the winter break, she *auto-ported* back to the island every year, just to attend the bonfire. It was usually a party she wouldn't miss.

After the exhausting day delivering Haloa gifts and the emotional experience of playing with Eugenia's nieces, though, she almost decided not to go. She was feeling better, but she still wasn't up to being social.

A small voice in the back of her mind reminded her that it wasn't all about the party. And that it wasn't all about her.

The mental debate didn't last long. Minutes later she was on the beach.

She was glad she came.

With the sand beneath her feet and the stars above her head, she felt the roller coaster emotions of the day fade away.

The beach was busy enough that she could find a quiet spot off to the side to be alone with her thoughts without drawing anyone's attention. Everyone else was too busy celebrating to notice.

For the first time in almost a year, Adara didn't resent them. She didn't envy them. She didn't want to join them, but she was happy for them.

A short while later, Adara saw Phoebe arrive with Stella, Nicole, and their friend Troy. As Phoebe's gaze scanned over the crowd, Adara knew she was looking for her.

And she was surprised to find that it didn't bother her.

A lot of things had changed that day.

When Phoebe crossed the beach and dropped down onto the sand, Adara even smiled at her.

"Hey," Phoebe said with that cautious tone she had taken to using with Adara. "How are you?"

"Tired," Adara replied.

She could feel Phoebe' s relief at the friendly answer.

"Me too." Phoebe fell back against the sand, staring up at the night sky. "I could barely manage to lace up my Chucks."

She lifted her foot into the air, as if showing off her shoe-tying success, and then dropped it back to the sand.

Adara laid down on the sand next to her.

"I almost didn't come," she admitted.

Phoebe tensed for a moment, maybe trying to decide how to respond, and then said, "I'm glad you did."

They lay there in silence for a while. Adara stared up at the starry heavens and was reminded of a song from an animated movie she used to love. Somewhere, out there, her mother was sleeping underneath the same sky.

That thought helped her keep things in perspective.

Her mother was alive. She was out there, doing something that made her happy and that made the world a better place. One day, she would return, and Adara would be ready to welcome her home.

"You seem…" Phoebe began. "Better?"

Adara drew in a deep breath and let it out slowly. Their friendship was new and tender. She wasn't sure how much she was ready to share. "I am," she finally said. "I'm okay."

"Good."

"I'm not fine," she quickly explained. "I'm not sure I'll ever feel totally fine about this."

Phoebe reached over and took her hand. It probably shocked Phoebe as much as it shocked Adara when she didn't pull away.

"But I'm okay." She gave Phoebe a quick squeeze. "I'm going to be okay."

As they lay there, small white flecks began to fall from the cloudless sky. It took Adara several long seconds to realize what was happening. What *had* happened earlier that day.

"It was you?" she accused with a smile. "You made it snow this morning?"

Phoebe gave her an innocent smile. "Maybe."

"You really have gotten better control of your powers," Adara said, more impressed than anything else.

Phoebe squeezed her hand. "I had a good teacher."

As Adara lay there next to her friend as snow fell on the beach, she felt at peace for the first time in a long time.

NEW YEAR, NEW MERMAID

A FORGIVE MY FINS STORY

ONE

December 31, 3:58 PM

NEW YEAR'S EVE was going to be magical. Marina Borealis could feel it in her fins. As part of the Festival Court, she got to help decorate for all the balls and parties at the palace. New Year's Eve had to be her favorite. And not just because of the kelpaper streamers swooping from one side off the ballroom to the other, the bioluminescent starfish dotting the ceiling to look like a night sky, or the glitter-filled balloon bubbles that were timed to burst precisely at midnight, promising to fill the water in with a million tiny sparkles.

No, Marina loved New Year's Eve most of all because of the promise. The hope for change. The possibility that maybe things might finally be different. That *she* might be different.

On New Year's Eve, anything was possible.

Then again, she had been hoping the same thing for the last five years, and nothing had changed. Her dark waves hadn't magically turned golden blonde, her plain brown eyes still weren't that seagrass green color that she favored, and she was still woefully single. Her life was exactly the same.

She knew she wasn't the only mergirl in the sea to make a wish on the stroke of midnight. But she desperately wanted more than most for some unseen magic to grant her wish.

She kept hoping. As she helped the other members of the court, she mentally practiced her midnight wish.

This year, she had decided to narrow her focus. Maybe she had been asking for too much. Maybe too many changes all at once weren't possible. Whatever magical entity might grant her wish could have been confused by the laundry list of requests and just decided not to bother.

This year that would not be the case.

This year she would ask for only one thing. The one thing that truly mattered to her.

If there were a magical wish-granter out there, her desire would be crystal clear.

Marina grabbed a bucket of glowing starfish and swam for the ceiling. She couldn't let her daydreaming get in the way of her work. This was the fun part. The part before the social anxiety, before the stressing over boys and friends and clothes and makeup. This was bliss.

The orchestra was on the stage, practicing. Strains of classical Thalassinian music floated through the water. Marina hummed along with the music as she swirled herself in a random pattern to make sure the starfish didn't look too uniform.

"Hey, Marina," Zanzia Marlin called up, "have you seen the photo shell props?"

Marina pointed to the buffet table lining the back of the room. "I think they're under the cupcake tower."

Zanzia thanked her and swam off to find the silly hats and funny costumes.

There weren't many members of the Festival Court still working. Most had gone home to change for the party.

Marina lived close enough to the palace that she could work longer and still have time to get ready. She wouldn't leave until she was sure everything was perfect.

She was so lost in her own world of placing starfish that she didn't notice anyone swim up behind her until he was tickling her ribs.

"Aaccck!" she squealed and spun around. Her bucket of starfish swirled away, sending the glowing stars spiraling around the room.

Marina pressed her hand to her chest, where her heart was about to beat its way out. And not just because he'd startled her.

Caspian Palmata had the kind of smile that could make her forgive anything. Even scaring her half to death and making a huge mess. She'd forgiven him a lot more over the years.

"Gotcha." He winked as he darted down and caught her bucket before it swirled out of reach.

His golden hair swished around him like an anemone in a hurricane. It was longer than his mother usually let it get, but Marina liked it long. It made him look wild and untamable.

"I wasn't scared," she lied.

He smirked. "I can see your pulse pounding."

He reached forward and pressed his fingertips to her neck,

right below her jaw. A flash of heat flooded through her body. She opened her mouth to say something smart, but nothing came out.

He pulled his fingers away as if it had been no big deal. To Caspian it wasn't. He was just like that. He touched her all the time. Little, light gestures. Big bear hugs. Everything in between. It was just his way.

But to Marina the meant more.

They both started after the wayward starfish simultaneously, as if they'd spoken a plan out loud. After a dozen years of friendship, they didn't need to say the words.

"I thought you weren't coming," she commented as they swam down.

He shrugged, "Practice ended early."

"I'm glad you're here," she said.

He stopped swimming. "Are you?"

She frowned. "You're my best friend," she said. "Shouldn't I be glad to see you?"

His grin could have lit up the entire palace. The warm feeling his touch had ignited exploded into her chest.

"Did we get them all?" he asked, nodding at her bucket.

Marina checked. "I'm not sure. I think there is a big yellow one missing."

Caspian spun around, searching. A moment later, he ducked behind the ice sculpture of Poseidon and retrieved the last of the starfish. "Found the sneaky guy."

Marina held out her bucket as Caspian swam back to her. He stopped a few feet away and tossed the starfish at her. It missed the bucket by two feet.

"Honestly, I don't know how you're the star of the bubble-ball team," she teased.

"Cut me some slack," he said as he swam after the starfish. "I'm not used to shooting sea stars."

This time Marina reached out and took the starfish from him and placed it in the bucket. If she didn't, he would keep trying until he made the shot. Even if it took until next New Year.

"What can I do to help?" he asked.

Marina surveyed the room. "We're almost done."

"Once again, my timing is perfect."

Marina flashed him a sarcastic smile. "But you can help Otter move the glitter bubbles into place."

His smile wavered.

Last year one had exploded all over Caspian, covering him in blue, green, and silver glitter just moments before the party began. But he was never one to back away from a challenge. He probably knew she was testing him. He just rolled up his sleeves, swam down to the corner where Otter was wrestling with the netting that held the balloons down, and started helping.

Marina went back to placing the last of the starfish. She was just pressing the big yellow one to the very center of the room when Caspian called out, "Here, let me help."

For a second, Marina thought he was talking to her, that he was going to help her place the last of the starfish.

Maybe he wanted to be part of the crowning moment.

But when she looked, he was swimming over to Zanzia, who was wrestling with the photo shell. Caspian got there just in time before the thing would have crashed into the wall.

One they got it secured, Zanzia looked up at him with stars in her eyes. "Thank you," she told him earnestly, her cheeks tinted pink and her eyes fluttering. "It could have killed me."

Caspian laughed. "I doubt it, but I'm glad to be of service."

Zanzia laughed in return and then she reached out and placed her hand on Caspian's forearm. Marina felt her hands tighten around the bucket handle.

"Will you be at the party?" Zanzia asked.

Caspian winked. "Wouldn't miss it."

"I hope you'll save me a dance."

He took her hand, lifted it to his lips for a kiss. "I save all my dances for pretty mergirls."

Marina felt the blood in her veins run cold. The new year hadn't even begun, and already she felt her hope for a wish come true, a wish not yet spoken, drift away on the current.

Her best friend was a flirt. He had always been one. It didn't matter if the girl was sixteen or sixty-six, he flashed that charming grin and made them feel special.

Marina knew it didn't mean anything. His flirtations almost never went anywhere. It still hurt, but it was a pain she was used to.

If a lifetime of friendship with Caspian had taught her anything, it was that being in love with your best friend was the worst. When he didn't feel the same way, it was torture.

TWO

December 31, 6:13 PM

ONCE SHE WAS certain the party preparations were done and everything was set for a seamless night, Marina went home to get ready. As soon as she swam into her room, the exhaustion hit her. She floated down onto her bed and fidgeted with the ruffle at the edge of her blanket.

Why had she thought this new year would be different from any of the others?

She and Caspian had been best friends since guppihood. Their mothers had them on the same guppy league bubbleball team when they were four. They had been inseparable from day one.

Five years ago, shortly after Marina's twelfth birthday, something between them had changed. Not for Caspian. Everything had stayed just the same for him. He still saw her as his buddy, his bestie, his go-to for everything from headaches to homework.

But like magic, things had changed for her. One day Marina saw him as nothing more than her best friend, her buddy, her Caspian. And the next... she saw him in a completely different light.

He wasn't just a friend or a buddy. He was something infinitely more.

Immediately on the fins of that realization came another: he didn't feel the same way. To him, she was still nothing more than a friend. And as much as it hurt her to know that, it would hurt her a thousand times worse to lose that friendship.

She knew she would rather suffer a lifetime as his heartbroken friend than to lose him in her life altogether.

And so she had kept her mouth shut. She had never once told him how she felt. At every opportunity, she made a wish that he would be struck by the same magical change that had turned her world upside-down.

Apparently the magic had run out.

So she suffered in silence as he started going out with other mergirls. There had been a string of them. The popular captain of the bubbleball team was in high demand.

None of them ever seemed to be serious relationships. He took them to dances sometimes or out for pizza. They didn't last long. One day that would change, though. Marina didn't know if she could take it when it did.

She and Caspian had gone to a few dances together. As friends, of course. He still bought her a corsage and treated her like a date in some ways. But in others, she remained just a friend.

It was better than nothing. At least it used to be.

That was their plan for tonight's New Year's Eve party.

But for some reason, that thought brought tears to Marina's eyes. She kept picturing Caspian flirting with Zanzia. He would dance with the younger mergirl. Would spin her around and around on the dance floor, teasing and flirting and making her feel magical. And maybe at midnight, he would kiss her.

Marina had watched more flirtations and kisses than she could bear. She couldn't handle anymore. She couldn't stand seeing him in the arms of another, knowing that he would never be hers.

She couldn't do it this time.

Being just a friend wasn't a part she could play that night.

She floated up in bed and wiped the sparkling tears from her eyes. She had never been a very good liar. Especially not with people she cared about. The last thing she wanted was her brother asking why she was crying.

When she felt like there were no traces left of her tears and she had herself together enough to face Alec she floated downstairs.

She found him in the dining room, hunched over his pre-law textbooks. Like her, Alec had dark curls and brown eyes that had that soulful bookworm look. It took him several seconds to notice Marina in the doorway.

"You're not wearing your dress," her brother observed.

"They always said you were the smart one," Marina teased.

Forcing the humor into her words hurt, but not as much as her heartache.

A pair of frown lines creased his brown. "What's wrong?"

"Nothing," she said. That wasn't exactly a lie. Nothing was wrong. Nothing new, anyway. She was just done—done pretending, done suffering, done. "I don't feel like going to a party."

Alec floated up from the table. "Now I know something's wrong. You worked all week to make everything perfect."

"Exactly," she said, trying to divert his focus. "I'm exhausted. I just want to spend a quiet New Year's Eve at home. Is that against royal law or something?"

"No," he said slowly. "But it's not like you."

No, it was more like Alec. Her older brother was definitely more of the stay-at-home type. He was a looker, but until he got out from behind his stack of books, no one would notice.

He swam over and placed his wrist on her forehead.

"Are you sick?" he asked. "Should I bubble message Mom and Dad?"

"No, I'm fine." Her crush wasn't a reason to interrupt their parents' first vacation in years. "I just don't feel like it, okay?"

Alec studied her, looking for signs of illness or something. Marina stared him down until finally he shrugged and went back to his books.

The Royal College of Arts and Letters was on the complete opposite side of town. Alec had an apartment near campus, but he had come home to watch her while their parents spent two weeks in Costa Solara.

It was a good thing. If their mom were home, she would have seen right through Marina's facade. Thankfully her brother was already lost in his studying.

After digging through the kitchen for something to eat, she finally found a box of plumaria pudding. The food their mom had stocked in the kitchen before leaving was dwindling.

She must have forgotten how much Alec ate. Marina would have to convince him to make a grocery run.

Until then, Marina had to make do.

She had just floated into the living room, ready to choose a book from the shelf, when a message bubble floated in.

She sighed when she saw it was from Caspian.

Hey, are you ready yet? Maybe we can grab a slice before the party.

Her first instinct was to reply, *Sure.*

That had always been the way between them. Caspian came up with the plans, and Marina went along with them.

But something had changed in her tonight. No, *everything* had changed in her.

Maybe it was a flash of magic. Maybe it had been building up over the years, and she had finally reached her breaking point. Maybe it was because they were in their last year of school and she knew they would be going off to college soon. She had spent all of high school as the girl ridiculously in love with her best friend. She couldn't start college that way.

So instead of agreeing, she turned him down.

Decided to stay in. Quiet night with Alec. See you tomorrow.

As she watched the bubble float away, sending her refusal back to Caspian, she felt a mix of pride and sadness. Proud to have finally made a personal stand against her heartbreaking crush. And sad to think that maybe that was a sign of her giving up on it. On him. On *them.*

But better sad now than devastated later. The longer she held out hope, the worse the end would be.

She had to make herself move on.

After scanning every title three times, she finally found a

novel she hadn't read and plucked it off the shelf. As she settled onto the couch, a second message bubble arrived.

She had expected that. Caspian didn't like to be let down. He would beg and plead and tease her incessantly until she agreed.

Tonight, she would not relent.

She opened the bubble, already mentally composing her response.

Her jaw dropped slightly as she read the message.

Okay.

Just like that? He was letting it go without even a single plea? That wasn't like him.

Maybe he really was looking forward to kissing Zanzia at midnight and didn't want Marina there. Not that it ever bothered him before.

As she shoveled a spoonful of plumaria pudding into her mouth, she wondered if that meant something else had changed.

Maybe this new year really would be different. Just not in the way she'd always wished.

THREE

December 31, 6:39 PM

AFTER THE SECOND MESSAGE BUBBLE, Marina swam back up to her bedroom to read her book. Even Alec would know something was wrong if tears kept springing to her eyes.

She'd chosen a romance story, and from the first moment the couple met, she couldn't stop crying. If she was going to sob her way through the book, she didn't want her brother to see. He would only ask questions she didn't want to answer.

A happy love story was an odd choice considering her own love life was doomed to heartache. But something about reading tales of happily ever after made her feel better even as they made her feel worse.

She had just gotten to the part where the couple was having their first fight when the doorbell clanged.

Marina pressed the book to her chest, listening to see if she needed to get up.

"Mar!" Alec shouted up. "You have a visitor."

A visitor? That could only be one merperson.

She stopped at her mirror to wipe away signs of tears before heading downstairs. She wasn't surprised to see Caspian floating there.

He looked perfect. His shaggy golden hair had been slicked back with some kind of gel. He wore a classic black tuxedo jacket accented by a bow tie, pocket square, and cummerbund in seagrass green. They matched his bright eyes perfectly.

"What are you doing here?" she asked.

He scowled. "What kind of question is that?"

"I didn't mean it that way." She floated down into the front hall. "I thought you would be at the party."

"Without my best girl? Never."

Marina rolled her eyes. "I told you I wasn't going."

"That's why I'm here." He flashed her that grin. "To change your mind."

As he watched with hopeful eyes, she wanted to give in. She wanted to say, *Yes, okay, I'll go change.* Anything to spend more time at his side.

That was the Marina she had been for the last five years.

But she also knew what would happen if she did. They would go to the party. She would have fun for a while. Until Caspian started flirting with Zanzia again. Until she had to watch them dance up a whirlpool. Until she had to watch them kiss.

She couldn't do it. Not anymore.

It wasn't fair to him, she knew. But it wasn't fair to her either.

And so she surprised them both by saying, "No."

Alec, who had swum back into the kitchen before she came downstairs, floated into the doorway and gave her a shocked look.

She ignored him.

That her oblivious brother knew she was usually a pushover when it came to Caspian only strengthened her resolve.

"I told you," she said, swimming away into the living room. "I'm exhausted."

"You spent all week working on the decorations," he countered. "Don't you want to see the fruits of your labors?"

She did. Of course she did. But at what cost?

"I'll see the pictures in the Daily Royal."

She traced her fingers along the rows of spines.

Caspian swam up close behind her. "That's not the same, and you know it."

She could feel the heat of him all along her back. It took all of her willpower not to float back into him, to let him wrap his arms around her waist and convince her to give in to the entire night.

"No."

He swam closer still, until his lips were right next to her ear.

"Please," he whispered. "Please, please, please. It won't feel right without you."

She closed her eyes and drew in a deep breath.

She knew what he meant. They did everything together. They took the same classes, they joined the same clubs, they planned to attend the same college.

Telling him no, deciding to spend even one holiday apart,

felt wrong. It felt like the entire ocean was an upside-down swirl. But so did being in love with someone who didn't feel the same way.

Finally, after a long pause in which she actually considered giving in, Marina shook her head.

"I…" She squeezed her eyes against the tears that threatened to fall. "I can't."

She braced herself for the onslaught. More begging, more pleading, some coercion maybe.

She could handle it.

She was prepared.

The heat of his presence drifted away.

"Okay."

She wasn't prepared for that.

She spun to face him. "What?"

"Okay." He shrugged and gave her that little boy smile that she first saw on the bubbleball court all those years ago. "Let's stay in."

Marina blinked for what felt like several minutes.

"I didn't mean you—"

"I know," he said, spinning away from her. "But if you're staying in, so am I."

She watched, stunned, as he floated over to the couch.

"I have one condition though." He sank into her father's favorite chair. "We have to order pizza. I am literally dying for a slice."

Marina laughed. "Literally?"

Caspian pressed a hand to his tuxedo-clad stomach. "Literally."

He looked into her eyes from across the room. For a few

moments, she felt frozen. There was some kind of weight in that look, some kind of seriousness that Caspian tended to avoid. He wasn't the serious kind. He played things off as a joke. Everything was fun for Caspian.

His seriousness made her fins itch.

Noise from the kitchen broke the moment.

"Okay," she said, warming up to the idea of spending the evening on the couch with Caspian. "I'll place the order."

He grinned and started loosening his bow tie.

As Marina swam over him, heading for the bubble messenger in the kitchen, he playfully tugged her tailfin. She felt it all the way to her ears.

When she got into the kitchen, Alec was waiting for her.

"You aren't seriously staying in?"

She pulled the pizza menu out of the drawer by the fridge. "I am."

Under her breath, she added, "We are."

She studied the menu and started mentally preparing their order. Caspian didn't care about food, as long as there was plenty of it, so he always ate whatever she ordered.

Alec floated to her side.

"I know how it feels."

"How what feels?"

When Alec didn't reply, she looked up. He nodded his head toward the living room, where Caspian was digging through a stack of sports magazines.

"That," he said.

Marina didn't think she understood. Or maybe she didn't want to.

"Did you know I've been in love with Lorelei Lamprey since I was six and she was four?"

Marina could only blink. Lorelei was one year older than her. They were next door neighbors, and the Lampreys had been family friends since before any of them were born.

Marina had never had a clue that her brother had a crush on Lorelei.

He gave her a sad smile. "You're not the only one who's good at hiding their feelings."

Marina couldn't keep her eyes from flicking to the living room. "Is it—"

"Obvious?" Alec finished. "Of course not. But I've known you your whole life. I'm more observant than you think."

She shook her head.

"I just… I can't anymore," she whispered.

Alec nodded. Then he placed his hands on her shoulders.

"This is the last New Year's Eve of your high school lives," he said, sounding far wiser than his three extra years should have made him. "You have the prettiest dress I've ever seen hanging on the back of your door. And your best friend is ready to chuck it all to stay home with you. Let the night be magical."

Marina looked at Caspian, lying on the couch, reading a magazine while wearing a tuxedo. Then she thought of all the hard work she'd put in that week. The decorations and the planning and the coordination.

Did she really want to miss out on all of that just so she didn't have to watch Caspian flirt with someone else?

Did she really want to make him miss out on the biggest party of the year for the same reason?

She wrapped her arms around her brother in a big hug.

"Thank you," she whispered. Then, because she couldn't help herself, she asked, "Why haven't you ever told Lorelei how you feel?"

Alec laughed and gestured at the living room. "Why haven't you?"

"Fair enough." She planted a quick kiss on his cheek and then pushed away.

She floated into the living room, hovering above Caspian on the couch. If he knew she was there, he didn't show it. She grabbed the top of the magazine and pulled it down.

"Pizza on the way?" Caspian grinned.

His smile fell when she shook her head.

"Let's go," she said, half regretting the words as she spilled out of her. "Let's go to the party."

"Yes!" Caspian twisted off the couch in a flash.

As he started for the door, Marina said, "Wait! I have to get changed."

The way his eyes raked over her made her shiver from head to fin.

"Why?" he asked. "You look beautiful already."

Marina felt the heat of a blush burn her cheeks. Caspian threw out compliments like that all the time, but for some reason tonight that felt different. Maybe it was just that she felt different.

Either way, it took her a moment to regain the ability to think and speak.

"Obviously," she said with forced sarcasm. "But if I don't wear the very expensive dress my mom bought me, I'll never hear the end of it."

His eyes sparkled. "Okay, then. Hurry up! We don't want to miss the shell drop."

As Marina darted upstairs, her heart fluttered like that time she'd brushed up against an electric eel. She couldn't put her fins on why, but maybe Alec was right. Maybe tonight would be magical.

FOUR

December 31, 7:48 PM

MARINA RARELY WORE DRESSES. Her tailfin tended to get tangled in the skirts, which made dancing, swimming, or even moving in general more difficult.

But the moment she had tried on this one—a seagrass green, ruffled and layered dream that the royal dressmaker recommended—Marina had felt like a queen. No wonder Princess Waterlily loved Mrs. Wentletrap's gowns.

Now, pulling it on for real, with the intention of wearing it out into the world for others to see, Marina felt anxious. She wasn't used to wearing anything more than a tankini top and, occasionally, fin guards during bubbleball games. She felt awkward.

Her mother always said, *Beauty comes from within, but it never hurts to add a little polish to the package.*

Floating in front of her mirror, Marina wove her hair into several braids and then twisted them up into an easy but elegant updo. It paid to have a mother who ran a multi-kingdom beauty business.

She pulled open the vanity drawer and started selecting her makeup. Tonight was a super special occasion, so her normal no-makeup routine wouldn't cut it.

She selected a juicy peach lip gloss and matching blush. After swiping an extra-black mascara across her lashes, she dabbed some of her mom's favorite rainbow highlighter over her cheeks and brow bones.

As she set the highlighter back in the drawer, Marina evaluated herself in the mirror. She wasn't nearly as skilled as her mom, but she felt transformed.

She felt… beautiful.

Marina laughed at herself. It felt weird to call herself beautiful. She was usually described as cute and maybe pretty. But tonight she felt truly beautiful. Inside and out. Her mom would be proud.

"Nothing left to do," she told her reflection.

On her way to the door, she grabbed the small beaded wristlet that perfectly matched her dress.

She floated downstairs, the chiffon layers of fabric trailing behind her like a train of jellyfish tendrils.

Alec saw her first. His eyes grew wide, and he let out a low whistle.

That drew Caspian's attention. When he turned to face her, his jaw literally dropped.

Their reaction made Marina blush. But it also made her feel powerful. Magical.

"You look…" Caspian floated toward the base of the stairs, meeting her as she reached the sea floor.

"Like an angelfish," Alec finished for him.

Marina smiled at her brother's exaggeration, but she couldn't look away from Caspian. His eyes were bright and shining and focused so intently on her that she felt trapped by them. Hypnotized. The longer he held her gaze, the more she grew afraid of what she might blurt out.

She forced herself to turn away, toward her brother.

Alec just shook his head with a stunned expression on his face. "Mom will be so impressed."

"You don't think it's too—" Marina fidgeted with her hair.

Alec shook his head. "It's not too anything." He floated forward and kissed her cheek. "Let me get the camera. Mom will definitely want a record."

He went into the kitchen to find the family camera, leaving Marina alone with Caspian. She didn't look at him again, she couldn't, but she felt him looking at her.

"Hey look, we match," he said.

He lifted up one of the ruffles from her dress up and held it next to the silk square tucked into his jacket pocket.

Marina forced a small laugh. It may have seemed like a coincidence, but she had gone tux shopping with Caspian. She recommended the green to him, the same bright green as his eyes.

She picked her gown to match.

"It's…" She reached out to touch the fabric of his pocket square, brushing her fingers over his in the process. "Yeah."

"Here we go," Alec said as he returned with the camera. "Let's take one of you floating down the stairs."

Marina hoped her makeup hid her blush as she swam back up and floated down for the camera. Alec took dozens of pictures from every angle, always insisting that he needed just one more. Now she knew what supermodels felt like.

It was starting to feel like a job until, after what felt like ten thousand shots, he said, "Let's get some of the two of you together."

He made a gesture, indicating that Caspian should move closer. Marina scowled at her brother and his blatant maneuver. He winked at her from behind the camera.

Two could play that game. Now that she knew about Alec's feelings for Lorelei, she could return the favor.

Then Caspian moved closer, and her thoughts froze. He wrapped an arm around Marina's waist and held her to his side. She leaned into him, unable to hide her blissful smile.

If nothing else ever developed between them, she would always have that night. She would always have that moment.

"Perfect!" Alec declared. "You two kids better get going if you're going to make it in time."

"Thanks, Dad," Marina teased.

She swam forward and gave her brother one more hug.

"Thank you," she whispered sincerely.

"Don't forget," he replied, leaning back and holding up the camera screen for her to see. "Let the night be magical."

The camera showed the last picture of the bunch, the one where Caspian had his arm around her. Only instead of his smiling face staring at the camera, his entire focus was on her.

It almost looked like he was the one in love with her instead of the other way around.

She knew what Alec was trying to imply. But he was wrong. He was seeing things that weren't there. Wasn't he?

A sliver of doubt crept into her certainty. What if…?

"Do we have time for food?" Caspian asked, yanking Marina out of her thoughts.

"Maybe," she said, "if we—"

"Never mind," he said. "There's food at the party. I don't want to miss the shell drop."

Marina kissed her brother on the cheek and then started for the door.

Caspian beat her there and held it open for her. As they swam out into the night, her brother's words echoed in her mind.

Let the night be magical.

She would try.

FIVE

December 31, 8:32 PM

As they swam away from her house, Caspian was unusually quiet. He was always the chatty one. Talking about the latest thing to grab his interest, asking a million questions, or just commenting on the weather.

But as they swam along the path that led to the palace, he didn't say a word.

There was a weird tension in the water. Marina couldn't quite figure out what it was. Was it coming from her? Was Caspian worried about something? Were they both anxious?

Not knowing what was causing the tension only made her tenser.

As they reached the outer edge of the palace wall, she couldn't stand it anymore.

With Alec's words echoing in her mind and the weirdness between them promising to make the night miserable if she didn't do something about it, she pulled to a sudden halt.

Caspian pulled up immediately, as if he'd been expecting her to stop.

Still, he said nothing.

They floated there, just outside the palace gate, staring at each other. Marina tried unsuccessfully to read the thoughts behind his seagrass green eyes. Either those thoughts were as muddy as her own, or they were shielded from her view.

All she knew was that something was wrong.

As they stared at each other, a strange feeling washed over her. The image of that last photo flashed in her mind. The look in Caspian's eyes. She decided that maybe nothing was wrong. Maybe something was right. Or maybe it was about to be right. For the first time.

Let the night be magical.

If this New Year's Eve, the last of her high school career, was going to be magical, then she was going to have to do something to make it magical. It wouldn't be magical all on its own.

Something had to change.

After several long years of pining and wishing, Marina knew that if she didn't take action, things between her and Caspian would never change. She would sentence herself to a lifetime of heartache.

Let the night be magical.

Caspian opened his mouth, as if he was finally going to say something.

Marina didn't give him the chance. She flicked her fin, floated close enough to feel his breath, and pressed her lips to his.

For the space of the heartbeat, nothing happened. They

both froze. Eyes squeezed shut, Marina narrowed her entire focus down to the pressure of the kiss. To the sparks that radiated out through her body, making her feel more alive than ever before. She wanted that feeling to last forever.

She knew it wouldn't.

At any moment, Caspian was going to snap out of it and shove her away. He would ask her what the frog she was doing and why she was doing it. She had to feel every sensation while she could. She wanted to burn every ounce of the kiss into her memory. It would be the only one she ever had.

She let her entire being melt into their joined lips even as she braced for the end.

Everything seemed to happen at once.

Caspian's arms came around her waist. Hers went instinctively around his neck. His head tilted slightly to the right and pressed forward, locking their lips tighter together.

When his hands came to either side of her face, she expected him to finally push her away. Instead, his fingers dug into her hair and pulled her closer.

Tears stung at Marina's eyes as she realized he was kissing her back. He was kissing her back.

She squeezed her arms tight around him.

His lips were pillow-soft, but firm, and felt like fire against hers. She was ready to let them burn her alive.

Nothing else mattered.

Caspian Palmata was kissing her back.

SIX

December 31, 8:39 PM

TIME STOOD STILL.

As Caspian's mouth moved over hers, and hers over his, Marina could feel the sparks of magic around them. The rest of the ocean faded away. They were the only two merfolk in the world, as far as she was concerned.

When he finally broke off the kiss, it felt like he took part of her with him. Her mouth tried to follow, desperate to get that part back. But he held her away.

He pressed his forehead against hers. They were both breathing hard. Marina knew it wasn't just the kiss that made her lungs draw in desperate ragged breaths of water. It was also the exhilaration of five years of longing and anticipation finally coming true.

When she had recovered enough to speak, Marina opened her mouth to... What? To apologize? She wouldn't. To explain? She wasn't sure she could.

In the end, it didn't matter because Caspian spoke first.

"You have no idea how long I've been waiting for you to do that," he said with a crooked smile.

All of the words that were on the tip of her tongue just floated out into the Gulf Stream. "What?"

He removed one hand from her hair and trailed it down her arm, leaving little sparks along the way. He entwined their fingers together.

He stared at their joined hands. "I've been head over fins in love with you since the fifth grade."

For the longest time, Marina could only blink at him.

His words did not make sense. They couldn't.

"What?" she gasped again. "*What?*"

He finally lifted his eyes to look at her. They were completely open; his emotions laid bare. Nothing was shielded from her now.

She could see it. The love. The same love she'd felt for him for the last five years. And he'd felt it for the last seven?

She couldn't wrap her mind around the possibility.

"Y-you never said a word," she stammered. As she spoke, she realized the statement also applied to her. She had been feeling the same way but hadn't told him how she felt. She had been too afraid of the consequences. Was it so hard to believe that he'd been afraid of them too?

"There were times," he said softly, "when I thought maybe you wanted more than friendship."

He huffed out a small laugh, like he was laughing at himself.

"But then I thought, what if I was wrong?" he continued.

"What if I told you and it made you uncomfortable? What if you didn't even want to be friends?"

It was like he took the words straight out of her brain.

Marina pressed her hands to his cheeks. "I felt the same."

His eyes filled with the same hope that she felt lifting her up toward the surface. After five long years, it was like the world around her had finally exploded with promise and possibility.

"Since seventh grade," she continued. "I felt the same. I feared the same."

He stared into her eyes, like he couldn't quite believe what she was saying. That made two of them. But now that she had finally said the words, they felt like the most natural thing in the world.

"I can't believe we both—" She shook her head. "How did we not know?"

"We were both idiots." He took one of her hands and pressed his lips to her palm. "We've wasted a lot of time."

"That doesn't matter," she said. "What matters is that we don't waste any more."

With that, she pulled him in for another kiss. She poured everything she had into it, all the years of longing and wishing and heartache. And she felt all of those same things pouring out of him. It was as if they had both been released from self-imposed prisons and were finally, irreversibly free.

Marina wanted to both laugh and cry with the joy of it.

Some time later he finally dragged his lips away.

Their breath mingled in the water between them.

"Do you still want to go to the party?" he asked.

"Do you?" she replied against his mouth.

He leaned back. "Well, we did get all dressed up."

She glanced down at their matching formal wear. "It would be a shame to waste all this fanciness."

He took her hand and started for the gate. "Plus, I don't know about you, but I'm ready to make everyone jealous."

"Me too."

As they swam, he said, "Happy new year, Marina."

She glanced at the clock on the palace's main tower.

"It's not new year yet."

He looked back at her with a grin. "It feels like it. It feels like a whole new year."

She smiled back. "I know. It feels like a whole new life."

Dear reader,

Thank you for reading *Myths and Mistletoe*, my very first holiday story collection. I hope you loved it!

Do you know the best present you can give an author? Reviews! They really help new readers find their books. So if you enjoyed these stories and want to see more of them in the future, please leave a review at Goodreads and your retailer of choice.

To get free stories, bonus extras, and breaking news, visit teralynnchilds.com/subscribe to sign up for my mailing list.

If you fell in love with these characters and their worlds, flip the page to find out more about the series they came from...

Tera L. Childs

If you loved Of Solstice Dreaming...

Find out how Winnie and Cathair's magical romance began in
When Magic Sleeps, the first book in the Darkly Fae series.

If you loved A Mythmas Carol...

Read all about how Gretchen, Grace, and Greer first met and
got their mythological-monster-hunting start in *Sweet Venom*.

If you loved Snow Falling on Serfopoula...

Get the scoop on Adara's nemesis, Phoebe, and how she
wound up at school on a tiny Greek island in *Oh. My. Gods.*

If you loved New Year, New Mermaid...

Dive into more mermaid romance in *Forgive My Fins*, which
stars princess Waterlily Sanderson and her biker boy neighbor.

ABOUT THE AUTHOR

TERA LYNN CHILDS is the award-winning young adult author of books about myths, mermaids, and magic, including the mythology-based Oh. My. Gods. series, the Forgive My Fins mermaid romances, the kick-butt monster-hunting Sweet Venom trilogy, and the Darkly Fae series. She currently lives in Las Vegas and spends her time writing wherever she can find a comfy chair and a steady stream of caffeinated beverages. Find her online at *teralynnchilds.com*.

MORE BY TLC

the Oh. My. Gods. series

Oh. My. Gods.

Goddess Boot Camp

Goddess in Time

the Forgive My Fins series

Forgive My Fins

Fins Are Forever

Just For Fins

the Sweet Venom trilogy

Sweet Venom

Sweet Shadows

Sweet Legacy

the Darkly Fae series

ACKNOWLEDGMENTS

A very special thank you to my editor, Bev Katz Rosenbaum, for getting her insightful notes to me practically overnight. This project wouldn't have made it on time without you!

55515520R00102